The gray film continued to spread through her mind and cloud her visions. Her eyelids grew heavy. She lowered to the ground and lay on her back. The blue sky above lost its vibrant colour as the world around her closed in. Her heart slowed. Her breathing grew shallow.

A man stepped over her and peered down, his bulk blocking out the last of the light. Shadows obscured his face but not the long dagger he held perilously close to her body. His other hand reached up to his ear. Did he have a phone? An earpiece? Her vision wavered and continued to close off.

"Camhanaich," the man said, his voice low and growly.

"We have a problem."

Praise for novels of J. C. McKenzie

Shift Happens

"SHIFT HAPPENS has excitement, intrigue and lots of danger. I love the whole cast of characters and how they played a part in the story" —*Fresh Fiction*

Beast Coast

"I loved this book as much as the first. There are secrets, surprises, and all manner of supernaturals." —*Paranormal Romance Guild*

Carpe Demon

"The story keeps the adrenaline pumping and spine tingling tension building throughout the story with well written scenes full of vivid details that capture the imagination and make it easy for the reader to become engrossed..." —*Literary Addicts Book Community*

Shift Work

"It's a terrific series and if you like supernatural reads, with a side of romance, the sort with solid and intense plots, gripping and very real dangers, hard choices, supernatural people some of whom can be selfish, cruel and bloodthirsty...You'll be hooked." —*Jeannie Zelos Book Reviews*

Beast of All

"This time out, J. C. McKenzie has outdone herself with high-velocity action, soul deep emotions and one of those finishes that you want to replay over and over!" —*Tome Tender*

Books by J. C. McKenzie

NEVERMORE

A RAVEN CRAWFORD NOVEL, BOOK TWO

J. C. McKenzie

COPYRIGHT INFORMATION

Nevermore

COPYRIGHT © 2019 by J. C. McKenzie

Contact Information: jcmckenzie@jcmckenzie.ca

Cover Art: Eerilyfair Design
Raven artwork: Soner Bakir
Raven in nest artwork: Chad Keith

Publishing History:
First JCM Publications Edition, 2019

ISBN: 978-1-9992394-2-8 (print)
ISBN: 978-1-9992394-3-5 (ebook)

To the pub girls

You know who you are and
I'm so thankful to have you in my life.

Author's Note

It's the Canadian disclaimer again... Fair warning, I'm Canadian, and because this story is set in Canada, I will be subjecting you, the fabulous reader, to the wonderful, and sometimes confusing, world of Canadian spelling.

We use a combination of British and American spelling in the True North. It's "colour" not "color" and "organization" instead of "organisation." We love the letters U and Z, and have a fondness for the double L.

Also of note: Although we are technically a metric nation, our proximity to our American neighbours (see how I spelled that?) means we are well versed in the imperial system. Many of us still use feet and inches to describe our height and pounds for our weight. I'm not being inconsistent in my world building, I'm being realistic and reflective of the community I was born and raised in.

Canadians...we're complex and full of layers.

Like a tasty red velvet cake.

"Ah, distinctly I remember it was in the bleak
December;
And each separate dying ember wrought its ghost
upon the floor.
Eagerly I wished the morrow;—vainly I had sought
to borrow
From my books surcease of sorrow—sorrow for the
lost Lenore—
For the rare and radiant maiden whom the angels
name Lenore—
Nameless here for evermore."

~ Excerpt from *The Raven*, by Edgar Allan Poe

Chapter One

"It's not denial. I'm just selective about the reality I accept."

~ *Bill Watterson*

O f all the diners, in all the towns, in all the realms, he had to walk into hers to waste her time. Raven shifted her weight from one foot to the other to relieve the ache shooting up her legs. She took a deep breath and winced. A musty smell permeated from the worn carpet, concealed partially by the frying meat in the kitchen and the booze wafting off most of the customers.

Ah. Dan's Diner at its finest.

"I'm sorry." The customer at table eight peered up at her with large brown eyes, crinkled with laugh lines. "I don't have enough for a tip."

"That's okay." She brushed a long strand of black hair from her face. *Oh, here we go.* Insert sob story. It wasn't that Raven was unsympathetic to those without means. Quite the opposite. If anyone understood debt and poverty, it was Raven. But if she couldn't afford a sit-in meal plus the tip, she didn't eat out. Raven forced her mouth into a tight smile and hoped it came across as reassuring to the customer despite her sinking stomach.

In Canada, servers earned minimum wage with the assumption they'd make up the difference with tips earned from hustling their butts. But that wasn't really the issue. If it was just a lost tip, Raven wouldn't feel so bitter. Most places, including Dan's Diner, required servers to pay a certain percentage of their total sales, called a tip out, to the non-serving staff. Technically, if a table stiffed her on a tip, Raven lost money because she had to tip out no matter what. This meant she made less than minimum wage. That's what ground her gears.

She knew her limits and played within it, why couldn't everyone else?

"I have something better." The man smiled.

Oh no. A phone number from a middle-aged, balding man sporting a dad sweater was not adequate compensation. This Saturday graveyard shift kept getting better and better.

He reached into his tight hipster jeans—the kind indicating he had more money than fashion sense in addition to delusions of his age—and pulled out a jewellery box.

Raven's eyebrows shot up. This was a new one.

"You can pick any gem in the box."

Raven groaned. On the inside, of course. No need to be rude or completely forgo a gratuity. She might be a less-than-stellar waitress, but she wasn't an unprovoked asshole.

"Some are quite expensive," he said.

"I'm sure they are." The only thing Raven was sure of was this guy probably picked the trinkets up at a dollar store. The corner of her right eye twitched. She shifted her weight on her feet again. She needed to think up a polite excuse to flee before something snarky erupted from her mouth.

The man opened the jewellery box.

Oooo. Shiny. Her Dark Other energy pulsed inside her. The birds wanted out.

As a part-fae raven shifter, she loved shiny things, and all intention of escaping flew away the moment Dad Sweater lifted the lid.

Under the stark diner lighting, various hues of blue, gold and pink sparkled from the gems sitting in the velvet interior of the jewelry box. One less-than-shiny stone sat off to the side. Instead of the light dancing off its black surface, it seemed to draw in the questionable diner lighting, absorbing it while still giving off a captivating lustre.

She rubbed her clammy hands on her black polyester pants and bit her lip. The more she stared at the gem, the more she wanted it.

Take, her ravens whispered.

Should she touch the black stone?

No.

She shook her head. No, she shouldn't.

She leaned in and reached out to touch the odd, pear-shaped gem. She stopped.

"Ah..." The man nodded. "The black spinel. Excellent choice." He plucked the jewel from the box.

Raven held her breath, tracking the gem with her gaze, every bird inside her alert and ready to burst forward.

He rolled the black spinel to sit on his weathered palm and held out his hand. "It's yours."

Raven gently collected the gem from his hand, pinching it between her forefinger and thumb. It was a larger jewel, pear-shaped, with lots of facets.

Once, back in her delusional days when she dated a compulsive liar but hadn't figured out his character flaws yet, she'd researched diamonds, cuts and rings, dreaming of becoming Mrs. Robert Fleming. Ugh. She avoided becoming Mrs. Douche but what cut the deepest was the relationship ended on his terms, not hers.

Robert had done her a favour, but she still wished she'd broken his heart, not the other way around.

"It has one hundred and forty-five facets," the man said.

Raven shook herself from her funk. "Sorry, what?"

"Normally, a pear cut gem has around fifty-eight. This beauty has more than double."

Raven held the stone up to the light. The black faces mesmerized her. She clutched the pretty rock and brought it to her chest. Though her white blouse provided a thin, synthetic barrier between her and the gem, the rock *felt* right against her body, as if it contained energy of its own and meshed with hers perfectly. "I've never heard of a black spinel."

The man snapped the jewellery box closed and pushed away from the table to stand. "It's a rare, single refractive stone, but it's gaining popularity. It also happens to be my favourite. Good choice."

Was he full of crap? Raven glanced down at the rock in her hand again. Despite the warmth of her hands, the gem remained cool. This could be some cheap plastic for bedazzling the butt pockets on preteen jeans for all she knew.

"Are you sure you want to part with it?"

"Absolutely. It's yours, *mo bhanrigh*." The pupils of his eyes bled out to cover the irises before retreating to boring brown.

Raven blinked. What in the Underworld was that? Had she imagined the eyes of an Other? Her Other senses hadn't detected anything. Her scalp wasn't prickling and her hair remained straight. Normally, it curled in the presence of Underworld energy.

"Mo what?" she asked. She must've imagined his eyes tweaking out. After all, she hadn't been sleeping well lately.

He smiled again and turned to walk out the door.

"Wait a minute!" Raven stalked after the man. Weird eyes or not, too much crazy shit had plunged into her life to let a mysterious, gem-toting man spouting words sounding suspiciously of the Underworld leave without an explanation.

"Waitress." A man growled as she walked by.

She ignored him.

"Waitress!" His wife reached out and snatched her serving apron.

Rip! The cheap material tore, and coins flew through the air, smacking tables and the floor in a clatter. Customers from nearby tables dove on the loose change like vultures. On their hands and knees, they filched her hard-earned tips.

"Hey! That's mine." Raven snarled at the customers.

The woman who grabbed her apron straightened in her seat and let go of the material. She lifted her hands in surrender, as if she wasn't responsible for this clusterfuck. Raven narrowed her gaze and barred her teeth. The husband squeaked. The vultures dropped the coins and backed away from the scene of the crime with wide eyes, like they hadn't just tried to steal loose change from a rundown waitress in a greasy spoon dive on a Saturday night.

The door chimed.

Raven turned to watch the front door close.

"Crap!" She ran to the entrance and flung open the

door.

The cool night air of North Burnaby greeted her. Gentle wind rolled through the nearly empty parking lot, rustling fallen leaves. The man had disappeared. Raven stood at the entrance and clutched the odd black stone to her chest.

"Raven?" Her brother Mike stood behind her. He must've come out of the kitchen when he saw her race by. Though nineteen and in his second year of university, Mike hadn't filled out his tall frame yet, and given the wiry, lean build of his father, he probably wouldn't. A thick mop of red hair hinted at his fox shifter nature and his kind eyes proved the harshness of their reality hadn't turned him into a bitter inhabitant yet. A grease-coated cast decorated the arm he'd broken while caught in a leg-hold trap a month ago. "You okay?"

"I'm not sure."

Chapter Two

"Remember, we all stumble, every one of us. That's why it's a comfort to go hand in hand."

~ Emily Kimbrough

Over-teased chestnut hair and a familiar face caught Raven's attention before she could run back into the diner to find out what those customers at table six wanted. The attractive woman stalked across the parking lot toward the restaurant's entrance. Her stiletto heels clacked against the dry pavement and sent echoes through the night. Well, early Sunday morning, now. A souped-up sports car playing loud music with the bass cranked too high drove past. *Boom, boom, boom.*

Where'd she know this woman from? If she wasn't wearing a scowl and stalking toward the diner with deadly intent, she'd be pretty.

Oh no.

Memory clicked in.

This couldn't be good.

The car with the loud music turned the corner and the music faded into the night, giving way to the punctuated clack of the woman's heels. A gust of wind blew through the parking lot, flinging Raven's black hair back. Though fall, the infamous rain of Vancouver and the surrounding areas hadn't started yet. When it did, it wouldn't stop for days.

The woman brushed her hair from her face without missing a step.

"I'm definitely not okay now," Raven told Mike, who still lurked behind her.

Mike peered over her shoulder, bringing with him the sweat and grease from the kitchen. "Who's that?"

"Robert's fiancée."

"Poor thing," Mike muttered.

Raven was inclined to agree except the other woman looked pretty pissed off and intent on confronting Raven.

"Do me a favour?" Raven asked her brother, without taking her eyes off of...what was her name? Sarah? That's right. Sarah. Robert had brought her to the diner once.

"Yeah?"

"Check on what table six wanted and pick up the change on the floor?"

Mike grunted. He hated covering tables. He hated "cleaning" even more. His room was a disaster.

"And if I'm not back inside in five minutes, come get me."

"You got it." Mike squeezed her shoulder before slipping into the restaurant. The door clicked shut behind him, cutting off the classic rock tunes straining from the static speakers and wafts of greasy meat.

Sarah screeched to a halt two feet away and vibrated with angry energy. The bright entrance lights illuminated her delicate features and the fevered gleam in her eyes. Her subtle floral scent laced with something slightly furry wound around Raven. Hmmm. The furry note was still there. She must be a shifter of some kind, but akin to inquiring about someone's ethnic background, asking a supernatural what type of shifter they were was considered rude.

"Sarah, right?" Raven said.

"Cut the crap."

Raven's mouth snapped shut. She narrowed her eyes at Sarah. She might've felt sorry for the woman the last time they met, being engaged to a sociopath and all, but nope. Not anymore. Raven's hands flew to her hips. She didn't owe this woman a goddamn thing. "The only one dishing crap right now is you. What's your problem?"

"You're his ex."

"Yeah, so?"

"The one he always talks about."

Ew, gross. "I talk about him a lot, too."

Sarah snarled. "I knew it. You're one of his whores."

The temperature dropped again as the wind picked up. Raven clutched her stone in one hand and used the other to rub her arm. Her hand slid against the cheap material of the blouse, but anything was better than reaching out and slapping the woman standing in front of her.

"I'm one of his victims," Raven said. "I talk about how much he fucked me over and how glad I am that he's no longer in my life."

Sarah rocked back on her heels. Her expression flattened, as if Raven's words slapped the attitude right off her face. "What?"

"I despise Robert. I want nothing to do with you or him, and I'm certainly *not* his whore." Raven stopped rubbing her arm. The rock pulsed in her hand while the smooth surface remained cool against her skin.

The woman's shoulders slumped. Her gaze cut to the side. "Oh."

"Oh?" Raven folded her arms over her chest. "Oh? You stomped to my place of work, yelled at me, called me a whore, and now all you have to say is oh?"

Sarah rubbed her arms as if subconsciously copying Raven. "I'm sorry. It's just that... It's just."

"Woman, spit it out. I have customers to ignore and tips to get stiffed on."

"I think he's having an affair." The woman's lip trembled.

You don't say? Raven swallowed her bitter laughter. She remembered the burn of finding out the truth of Robert's actions. The emotional damage was still raw enough for her not to be a complete asshole about the situation. "You're probably right. After he left me with his debt, I discovered just how little he valued our relationship. He was cheating on me the entire time we were together."

The woman's eyes widened. Then something happened—some change in her thoughts and emotions. Her gaze flashed under the bright lights. Her muscles tensed and her delicate hands balled into fists.

"He'll regret this," she snarled.

Raven raised a brow. "Oh, I sincerely hope he does." She turned to go inside. "Best of luck with that. I'm going ba—"

"And you're going to help me."

Say what? Raven whirled around. The loose dirt on the cement landing crunched under her shoes. Sarah's lips twisted into a cruel sneer. Her brows pinched in. Oh crap, she was serious.

"Look," Raven started. "I hate him with every fibre of my being, but it would take an officer two seconds to connect any crime involving Robert with the bitter ex-girlfriend he saddled with a mountain of debt." She'd already thought of ways to hurt him. Bear, her twin brother had offered, and so had Cole, her something-or-Other. At the end of the day, though, as good as the revenge would feel, Robert's punishment would be temporary; whereas the consequences of her actions would be permanent. She already let him affect her life more than once, she refused to give the asshat any more power.

Her stepdad, Terry, always said she couldn't put a price on a clear conscience. Well, actually, Raven could. About fifty thousand dollars. That's the debt Dr. Douche left her with.

She *had* to believe cosmic karma would eventually catch up with him and kick him in the proverbial sac.

"You don't have to do anything but find him." Sarah tucked a chunk of wavy hair behind her ear.

"Find him?"

"He's missing. I haven't seen him since Wednesday morning. I assumed he was shacked up with his mistress."

Not a bad guess. Robert never had the gonads to break up with Raven in person. He ran away and left her a letter full of drivel. Thinking about his poor-me words, even now, made her want to track him down and throat punch him.

"Did he leave a note?" Raven asked. Another gust of wind flung long strands of hair in her face. She pushed them away. Wind could be so annoying, yet, she yearned to fly off into the night and play in it.

"No. Who does that?"

"Robert. Robert does that. And is leaving without a note somehow better?"

Sarah paused. "I guess not."

"If he's missing, call the authorities."

Sarah shook her head. "He's done this before. He'll

be back tonight or tomorrow and say he pulled some double or triple shifts and crashed at the hospital. He already laid down some groundwork and told me it was really busy, and they were short staffed. He warned me he might not come home. I naively believed him the first time, but I won't be fooled twice. I went to the hospital and he wasn't there. I want to know where he goes and who he's with."

"Again, I'm sorry, but he's not my problem anymore." Raven shrugged and turned to leave for the warmth inside where she didn't have to talk about an asshole anymore. "My advice? Cut and run. But check your bank statements first."

"I can pay you."

Raven halted. Money? Her ravens perked up again. Greedy beasts.

"You're a private investigator, right? You find missing things, Robert told me. I'll pay you."

Raven turned to Sarah again.

She had lost her snarl, but her body remained tense. The furry tang in her scent intensified.

Well, why not? Raven dug out a card for Crawford Investigations from the undamaged section of her server apron. The corners were worn, and it had a few crease marks, but the name and number were legible.

"If you're serious about this, give the office a call on Monday and set up an appointment."

"But..."

"But I'm working my other job right now and don't have time to do a new client interview to get all the information. This is a professional business. There will be a contract. Rules. Expectations." Unfortunately, that cut both ways. Raven would remain professional instead of slapping this woman in the face when she got annoying.

"He's missing and probably cheating. What else do you need?"

Raven rolled her eyes on the inside. "I need you to call the office and set up a meeting."

"Can't you start looking for him now and catch him in the act?"

"No." Raven walked back into the restaurant. Sarah started talking again, but Raven ignored her and let the door cut her off. The air heavy with grease hit her face.

Mike looked up from table eight with wide eyes and a distraught expression, dirty dishes precariously perched on his limbs. A long coffee stain now decorated one leg of his kitchen whites.

"Help," he mouthed.

Chapter Three

"They say best men are molded out of faults, and, for the most, become much more the better for being a little bad."

~ *William Shakespeare*

Mike slid into the booth seat opposite Raven. The faux leather creaked, and air puffed out of the cushion when he plunked down and settled. He thunked his cast on the table.

Raven wrinkled her nose. The worn, grease-soaked plaster radiated a stench all its own and it wasn't pleasant. Surely, the cast had to be a health code violation, but Dan's Diner lived life on the edge like that.

"I don't know how you do it," Mike said.

Raven finished piling all her quarters and started working on the rest of the change. "I don't. If I was better at this crap, I wouldn't be working here."

"I guess the same could be said about my cooking." He waved his stinky cast at her. "But I only need one good arm to flip burgers."

Raven looked up from her measly stacks of coins. "Yeah, but you're different."

Mike rested his arms on the back of the booth, setting the stinky cast farther away from her sensitive nose. "How so?"

"You're only doing this to pay for school. You're going places."

Mike skewered her with a dark look.

Raven sat up. Her nineteen-year-old gamer brother was sweet and supportive with a side of occasional sarcasm and dubious hygiene. He rarely ever gave her dirty looks. At least not ones he meant.

"I hate it when you do that," he said.

"Do what?"

He sat up and leaned forward. "Talk down about yourself."

"It's called self-deprecating humour, and I'm freaking hilarious."

Mike grunted. He opened his mouth to say more when the bell above the diner's entrance jingled and the door swung open. A gust of early morning air laden with car grease and grime rushed in.

"Oh, for fuck's sake." Mike flopped back in his seat. "I thought you ditched this guy."

Beul na h-Oidhche gu Camhanaich strode into the fluorescent lighting of Dan's Diner to upbeat oldies blaring through the old speakers. Named in the language of the Underworld, which translated to "Mouth of the Night to First Light," or "Dusk to Dawn" for the regular non-fancy folk, the Lord of Shadows commanded the darkest elements of the night. Well over six feet, with broad shoulders and a muscular chest tapering to a narrow waist, Raven knew firsthand how good his body felt against hers.

Her mouth watered. She clamped her lips together and attempted to gather some willpower and dignity. *Focus, Crawford.*

Cole's dark Other gaze zeroed in on her, so dark the pupils appeared to bleed to the very edges of the iris, leaving only a silver outline.

Silver lining.

There had to be a joke in there somewhere, but nothing about the devastating assassin's presence inspired humour.

He wore his usual attire to blend in with mundane humans—dark jeans, and a blue hooded sweatshirt. He'd pushed up the sleeves to his elbows, exposing forearms corded with muscle. Those same arms had held her as he broke her world apart and put it back together again.

Crap. Was she drooling? She wiped her chin.

His features, too chiselled to appear pretty, gave his

handsome face a lethal, rugged edge. He was beautiful in the same way a jaguar stalking prey through a jungle or a pack of wolves hunting down an elk in a coordinated effort was beautiful.

The steel and oily grit of the North Burnaby night flooded in, but it also brought along Cole Camhanaich's unique scent—a seductive forest after sunset when the shadows grew larger than her avid imagination, and the darkness filled with sweet memories and the whispers of salacious promises.

In exchange for sparing her brother's life and protection for her family, Raven had agreed to work with Cole to reclaim stolen property. It turned out taking on the dark fae with only her wits and finely-edged snark wasn't her smartest plan, but she'd do anything to protect her family.

"Let me grab you a seat." Suzy, the waitress on the early morning red-eye shift, stepped forward, eyelashes fluttering.

She'd grab something, all right. Dan's Diner didn't have a "Wait to be seated" sign. She wanted to nab him as a customer before any of the other servers could.

Cole walked past Suzy without breaking stride or sparing her a glance.

Raven didn't dare look away. She couldn't even if she wanted to. There was something mesmerizing with the efficient way Cole moved.

Unlike others of his kind, his touch didn't dampen her power. With each step he took toward her, the dark energy she housed inside intensified and pushed for release. Her scalp prickled and even without a mirror, she knew her straight hair curled in the presence of the dark fae lord.

Mike snapped his attention back and forth between Raven and the Lord of Shadows, and groaned.

"Raven." Cole stopped a foot from their table. His low rumbling voice rolled over her like a thunderous wave.

She squeaked. Possibly in greeting, maybe in excitement, probably in anticipation.

Mike snarled.

Cole's gaze finally released her from its power and shifted to her brother. His expression remained blank. "Hello, Michael."

Her brother's gaze dropped to the four puncture wounds scarring Cole's forearm. Mike's snarl eased to a smug grin. He'd left those marks during a detour to break into their parents' house before heading to the emergency room. A night in which Raven hoped to never repeat again.

Cole's lip twitched. Apparently, Mike and Cole exchanged some non-vocal bro-code—Mike issuing a threat, and Cole acknowledging its receipt. Ridiculous, really. She loved her brother, but the fox shifter wouldn't last a second in a physical altercation with the patron fae of assassins and Cole wouldn't likely agree to some sort of computer hacking competition.

Cole tilted his head toward the kitchen.

Mike glanced at Raven, brows bunched.

She nodded.

Mike slid from the booth and stalked to the back of the restaurant. He wasn't even on shift anymore, but she appreciated the privacy. No one wanted to swoon or drool over a man in front of their baby brother.

Cole's intense gaze returned to her. "May I?"

Sweet baby Odin. That voice. Deep and gravelly, like a cross between a growl and the purr of a mountain lion, simple words coming out of that kissable mouth made her want to leap across the cheap laminate table and slap her body against his.

Cole slid onto the booth seat across from her.

"How've you been?" She bit her lip. After Raven killed Lloth, the Corvid Queen of Shadows, Cole took her home. Instead of letting him comfort her or take the opportunity to demand answers, she'd asked him to leave. Sure, during their search for her brother, he'd withheld information from her, but she kept evidence from him as well. Her need for space had more to do with her ignorance of the Underworld, the denizens within the Other Realms and how she fit into all of it.

Her choice, though sound, didn't stop her from dreaming of the Lord of Shadows. She woke up sweaty, frustrated, and rubbing against her sheets or her hand. She relived their time together over and over.

Her choice.

She'd never regretted a decision so much in her life. And that said a lot.

Cole leaned back in the booth and draped his arms over the seat. "Busy. Lloth's passing caused a lot of ripples within the Shadow Realm. You?"

Passing. What a nice and tidy euphemism for having her head clipped off and her body crunched in a giant bird's beak. Raven's stomach twisted. Memories flashed in her mind. Blood. Tissue. A sickening crunch. The burst of metallic fluid across her tongue.

She squeezed her eyes shut. *Don't think about it.*

What had Cole said? Lots of ripples? She nodded as if she knew exactly what those ripples were. She didn't. She had no clue. How had she been? "Busy."

Cole's gaze cut to the near empty diner.

"I moved home and I've applied to go back to college." Apparently, they now offered "mature student" grants. Hah! Talk about an oxymoron. It took Dad five minutes to stop laughing.

"Good for you." He smiled. The flash of straight white teeth mesmerized her. Last time he smiled, he'd faced three mercenaries intent on killing him and abducting her. This smile was different. This one was genuine.

Her heart ached, and her hand itched to reach out and hold his hand.

"How's Chloe?" His sister, also known as the *Claíomh Solais*, had been abducted along with her twin about a month ago. That's how she met Cole. They worked together to find and save their lost siblings.

"Good. How's Bear?"

The civility of this conversation might kill her. He wasn't here to trade pleasantries or ask about the twin brother he loathed. Bear had resumed his less-than-legal jobs after his safe return to the Mortal Realm, but he also made an effort not to be a selfish prick. She saw him, in person, more often now.

Her powers and conspiracy of ravens had strengthened with his presence and grown in numbers.

"Bear's good." She reached out and fiddled with the black gem sitting amongst a pile of quarters.

He leaned back and watched her, dark gaze twinkling under simple diner lighting.

"I have a giant metal scythe and no idea how to use it," she blurted. Cole had left her Lloth's weapon of choice before he disappeared from her life. She didn't understand why he'd leave such a valuable and dangerous weapon in her incapable hands. It sat in her bedroom, leaned against the wall with a bra or two hanging from the skull-emblazoned blade.

Cole's dark brows shot up toward his hairline. Humour tugged at his lips. "I also have a large...scythe. I'd be happy to show you how to handle it."

Raven choked and heat flared up her neck and face. Not going there. Cole hadn't graced her with his presence for sexual innuendoes or idle chitchat. Mike once accused her of getting distracted by Cole's dong. She needed to stay focused this time. "Why are you here?"

Cole leaned forward. His lips parted. His gaze snagged on the gem pinched between her thumb and forefinger. His brows furrowed. "Pretty rock. Where'd you get it?"

That's not what he'd planned to say. Why the change in direction? "Some customer," she answered.

His frown deepened.

"He called me mo bhanrigh. It sounded Gaelic or Underworlder. Know what it means?"

Cole stiffened. "Mo bhanrigh?"

"That's what I said." Naturally, he pronounced it exactly like the dad-sweater toting customer.

Cole shook his head, a small smile tugging at his lips.

He didn't shake his head because he didn't know. He shook it because he didn't plan to tell her. Grrr.

"Well?" she prodded.

"Well, what?"

"What's it mean?"

Cole's smile grew. He leaned forward again and reached out. He caught a lock of hair that had escaped her messy bun and let it slip through his fingers.

"I'll tell you," he said. "After dinner tonight."

"It's Sunday." Well, technically it was Sunday, but the early morning pre-dawn hours belonged to the night, so it still felt like Saturday to Raven. The clubbers had already come and gone, staggering out the doors to go home and sleep it off.

Cole straightened. "And you never miss roast night."

Raven grinned. "You've had my mom's cooking. Would you miss it?"

Something flashed across his gaze. His confident grin slipped to a smile, but not a happy one. Something about his expression seemed sad, as if he'd taken off a mask and let her glimpse a little of what lay beneath. In an instant, it vanished.

"No, *Einin*," he said. "I wouldn't."

Her chest warmed at his nickname for her. Little bird in Irish, according to Mike. "Did you..." She put the gem down amongst her sea of small change. "Did you want to come?"

As soon as the words left her mouth, the room darkened and grew warmer. The space between them closed as if by sheer willpower alone, Cole managed to shrink the room. Only the cheap table separated her from the beautiful man on the other side. The powerful and lethal dark fae lord she knew so little about, who still managed to make her blood sing. When she first saw him and before she learned his name, she'd called him TDD for Tall, Dark and Dangerous.

"Yes," he said. "I would."

Chapter Four

"I have never killed anyone, but I have read some obituary notices with great satisfaction."

~ *Clarence Darrow*

The doorbell rang and Raven's alcohol induced calm fled from her body like rats from a burning house. Behind her, somewhere down the hall and around the corner, Mike and their younger sister Juni argued about whether pineapples should be allowed on pizza while Mom puttered around in the kitchen. Cutlery clinked and dishes clanked, and the heavenly smell of roast beef wafted through the warm house.

Raven swallowed the lump in her throat and walked toward the front door. Why was she so nervous?

She wanted Cole. She wanted him so badly it hurt. What if he no longer wanted her? Her hair curled as she closed the distance to the front entrance, already responding to the dark fae energy on the other side. If Cole wasn't interested, why would he come to dinner?

Grow a pair, Crawford and keep your chin up. Raven heard Grandma Lu's voice as if the old woman stood right beside her instead of six feet under the ground.

She swung open the door.

Not Cole.

Her brain stumbled. Like a car on the highway with a failing timing belt, it faltered and turned over a couple of times before chugging along.

Her twin brother, Bjorn Crawford, stood on the landing, hand clasped with the beautiful woman standing beside him. Tall, wide and built like a professional swordsman, if that was still a thing, her brother earned his childhood nickname with his physical presence alone. Her brother's Otherworld magic brushed against her skin and bolstered her own power.

A month ago, another dark fae lord named Bane, hired Bear to steal the Claíomh Solais from Cole. When Bear discovered the "object of power" was actually Chloe, he refused to hand her over and tried to hide them both from the Lord of War instead. Somewhere in that process, the chronic dater fell in love with the dark fae woman and as far as Raven could tell, Chloe felt the same.

"Bear!" Raven beamed.

When her wayward twin "stole" from Cole, he started a chain of events that nearly cost them all their lives. Well, no. Not quite. The theft nearly cost Raven her life and everyone else their freedom.

"Hey, Rayray." Bear let go of Chloe Camhanaich's hand, stepped forward and enveloped Raven in his beefy arms. He gave the best bear hugs, but he wasn't named for them. Mom gave him a Scandinavian name to pay homage to her sperm donor's heritage—which, up until recently, was a complete unknown. The only information they gleaned from Mom was his "god-like" appearance. Bjorn and Branwen. Beautiful, well thought out names they both shirked for rather basic nicknames that in hindsight, might've been a bit too on the nose.

Mom was still sour on the name thing, and as it turned out, she wasn't too far off with the monikers she selected. Their biological father was Odin's two ravens, Huginn and Muninn, combined. Technically, this made both Raven and Bear grandchildren of the Allfather. Not that it mattered. First, no one had rolled out any red carpets for their royal footsteps to tread down.

And second, more importantly, Terry Crawford had married their mom when they were young and raised them as his own. He was the only dad they knew and the only dad they needed.

"Do I want to know why there's a goat in the yard?" Bear asked.

"That's Pepe," she answered.

"Of course, it is," Bear said.

"I'll let Dad tell you the story." She couldn't explain crazy and do it justice.

The goat in question bleated in the dark night. Raven peered out into the empty front yard. The cool autumn air brushed against her face. Did those shadows dance in the yard? She stretched and peered over Bear's bulky shoulders.

"Expecting someone else?" Bear asked.

"No, I guess not." She turned to Cole's sister and Bear's girlfriend, wrapped up in one stunning package. "Hey, Chloe."

"Greetings, Branwen." Her lyrical voice tinkled in the air between them like fairy bells. Her voice was as light and magical as her brother's was deep and seductive. The moonlight shone on her ebony skin and her silver white hair cascaded down her back like a waterfall made of unicorns.

No wonder Brother Bear was in love. Just seconds in her company and Raven questioned her own sexual orientation.

"Good to see you again." Raven opened the door and stepped back to let them in. "And please call me Raven."

The ravens perched outside croaked in the night.

"Yours or Odin's?" she asked.

"Mine." He winked before leaning down to give her

a quick peck on the cheek. He led Chloe down the hall toward the kitchen and dining room, his hand protectively placed against her lower back.

Bear had been a serial dater and a bit of a player before Chloe. He'd never brought a woman home to meet the parents. Ever. The only girlfriend they'd ever met was Megan and only because she was Raven's best friend. Luckily, their friendship survived the breakup aftermath.

But it hadn't ended well, and it hadn't been pretty.

"Hey, Mike!" Bear called out to their younger brother. "What do I have to bribe you with to release the hold you placed on my bank accounts?"

Mike grunted in response.

That's right. They'd frozen his accounts when he'd disappeared to flush him out of hiding to make contact with them. It hadn't worked. By then, the Corvid Queen already had her talons sunk into Bear and Chloe.

Raven continued to watch Bear and Chloe walk in perfect unison down the hall—like some sort of dance sequence, they seemed in time with each other. Dark energy from the Underworld bounced between them. As she continued to envy her brother's relationship, she shut the door.

Thunk!

The door hit something instead of clicking shut.

Huh?

She whirled to the entrance. A black combat boot stopped the door from closing. She swung the heavy door open and followed the foot up the powerful body to the face.

Her breath caught.

Cole stood on the threshold to her home. Though he wore a knit sweater with a collared shirt underneath and dark jeans, the night shrouded him like a cloak. The moonlight danced in his silvery dark eyes.

The air from her lungs escaped in a long sigh. "Cole."

"Einin." He stepped forward and caught a tendril of her hair. His full lips tugged at the corners. "I'm sorry I'm late."

Dark where his sister was light and pale where she wasn't, Cole and Chloe appeared as polar opposites, yet, their powers complemented each other, like some twisted sibling yin and yang from the Underworld. Cole controlled the shadows, and Chloe the light.

Cole let her hair slip from his fingers.

Her heart thudded. She licked her lips. "Come on in."

Cole strode into the house and his presence made her parents' hallway shrink and darken.

The Lord of Shadows sat on the bench in the hall by the door and methodically unlaced and removed his boots before placing them neatly on the mat. What a polite and house-trained assassin. He waited for Raven to close the door. She clicked it shut and waved for him to go ahead. He'd already been here for dinner and knew the way. Besides, if he went first, she could admire the view.

And what a view it was.

If she reached out, she could grab—

Cole stopped abruptly.

"Oomph." Her face smooshed into the softness of his sweater. She inhaled the sweet scent of the forest before rocking back. So fixated on his muscled thighs and ass in denim, she ran right into him. He stopped at the end of the hall where it opened to the kitchen and dining room.

Cole reached behind and held her steady. His large hand splayed against her lower back, hip and a portion of her butt. His dark energy vibrated through her jeans and shirt.

Heat raced through her veins at the familiarity and potency of his touch.

"Sorry," Cole's deep, hypnotic voice curled around her. "I didn't realize Chloe would be here."

Translation: he didn't know Bear was coming, and he didn't like it. In all fairness, no one knew Bear planned to grace them with his presence.

"Brother." Chloe beamed. The lights on the chandelier above the dining table brightened.

Cole removed his arm and hand from Raven, leaving her skin cool even under clothes. He walked into the dining room in time to catch his sister in a brief hug.

"Cole." Bear stood and offered his hand.

The Lord of Shadows looked down at her twin's offered hand as if it contained powdered anthrax.

"Cole," Chloe hissed.

Cole hesitated for another eon. He clasped Bear's hand. Luckily, they didn't try to compete for who had the strongest grip. A short brief shake and it ended. A collective breath released from the spectators, including Raven.

Bear held a seat out for Chloe. She beamed at Raven's brother and sat down.

Everyone else's heads snapped back and forth, watching Cole and Bear, as if watching a high stakes tennis match. Mike's eyebrows bunched as he watched.

"You can sit beside me, Cole." Juni batted her eyelashes. Fifteen going on fifteen, Raven's sister had learned little of subtlety or controlling her raging teenage hormones. She'd tamed her wild red curls and they framed her pixie-like face in a large halo.

Cole's smile returned. "Thank you."

"Stop standing around the table. Sit and eat." Mom walked in from the other room. From her flushed cheeks and watery eyes, Raven would bet her next shift's tips Mom left to collect herself after Bear sauntered in—with a date, no less.

"But Dad isn't home yet." Mike's point didn't stop him from taking a seat to dish a generous heap of mashed potatoes onto his plate.

"Mrs. Crawford." Cole stepped forward, took her hand in his own and bent to kiss her fingers.

Juni sighed, theatrically, somewhere behind Raven. At least she hoped it was her sister. Anyone else and that would just be weird.

Sweet baby Odin, the whole family was smitten.

"I'll get the extra chairs." Raven hadn't set a place for Bear or Chloe, but no one in the room would dare give him grief for not calling ahead. This was the first Sunday dinner he'd attended in over a year. If only she'd seen Mom's face when he first walked in. Her expression now was priceless.

Dressed in tastefully cut pants and a white blouse, Elizabeth Crawford looked more like a Stepford wife than the backbone of a fox-shifting skulk. Nothing of her polished exterior hinted at her wild child past. She'd partied hard, defied her parents and tested many boundaries, including the one between the Mortal Realm and the Underworld.

Currently, Mom stood in the kitchen looking as though at any moment she'd burst from happiness or break down in a flood of tears. Or both. She clasped her hands and watched them sit down. Her brood. Her skulk, even though Raven and Bear weren't fox shifters like the rest of them.

Mom's cheeks shone under the soft lighting and her red-rimmed eyes glistened. *Aww Mom*. Raven's twin always had a way of inspiring intense emotions in women, their mom was no exception.

"Where's Dad?" Juni asked.

"Surveillance," Mike answered between mouthfuls of roast beef and mashed potatoes. Savoury-scented steam billowed from the food in the dishes. Not only had he not waited for anyone to dish, but he'd taken Mom at her word and started eating.

Raven placed an extra chair on each side of the

table and took the one beside her twin. Cole dutifully sat on the other side across from her, sitting next to Juni. Her younger sister beamed.

Raven rolled her eyes and flapped her open hand at Juni. "Hurry up with the corn."

Her sister stuck out her tongue before handing over the bowl.

"This looks delicious, Mrs. Crawford," Cole said.

"Please, Beth."

Juni choked on her water.

Mike reached over and patted her back. Hard. Harder than necessary.

Juni glared at their brother.

Mike shrugged off the death stare, having already gained immunity from its potency from a lifetime of exposure, and returned to the food in front of him.

Geez, normally Juni had the insatiable appetite and poor table manners. Mike looked up from his plate and wiped the trail of gravy running down his chin with his shirt sleeve. He'd run a lot of surveillance for Dad, lately. Shifting required massive amounts of energy and burned a lot of calories.

He did a double take when he caught her staring.

"What?" he asked around a mouthful of food.

Chloe laughed. The tinkling bell-like sound chimed like fairies along Raven's brain cells.

Everyone froze. Then, in unison, they turned toward Bear's girlfriend, mouths gaping open.

Chloe's laugh cut-off and silence descended on the dining room. "Why is everyone staring at me?" She cast her large beautiful eyes at Bear.

Her twin frowned.

"Because." Mike swallowed his mouthful of food. "Because you're..."

"Beautiful." Juni's tone didn't carry the same awe as Mike's. Nope. Juni sounded bitter.

Raven sighed. Her sister was that awkward age where she was full of raging hormones that bolstered her confidence one moment and plagued her with self-doubt the next.

Chloe smiled. "Thank you."

Sitting next to Raven, Bear reached for Chloe's hand under the table and gave it a squeeze. Well, that was new. Not only had he brought home a girlfriend, but he made covert displays of affection. Next, he'd be making out in front of all of them.

Gross.

Cole glowered from across the table. He couldn't possibly see the under-the-table-hand-action, but he'd made no secret of his feelings regarding Bear's actions, or inactions, when they last met. He'd have killed her twin had they not made a deal. Right now, he looked as though he regretted that promise.

Chloe beamed at her brother, the brooding Lord of Shadows and everything changed.

His expression softened.

Maybe Raven didn't need to make a deal with Cole or worry about him breaking his promise. With one look from his sister, he backed off. He might've spared Bear anyway for Chloe's sake.

Huh.

"So, how's everything going?" Bear asked, randomly addressing the whole table.

Forks paused midair while everyone looked at each other.

Bear shifted in his seat.

He was trying. He was here. Odin's ball sack. Someone needed to say something.

"Well, I had a great day," Juni declared, apparently recuperating from her earlier jealousy-induced funk.

"And why's that?" Raven took a bite of creamy mashed potatoes. Warm buttery goodness coated her mouth. Yum.

"I finished the shampoo and conditioner at the same time. Do you know how hard that is?" Juni said.

Mike's eyes widened. "You need to get a life."

"Says the computer geek who lives in his room and flirts with a computer screen. I'll take my life over yours."

"I'm surprised you even notice what I'm up to with all that primping in front of the mirror," Mike said. "Hair's still a frizzball, by the way."

Juni's face turned red and she opened her mouth.

"Children!" Mom's hand slammed down on the table.

The front door opened and closed, the tell-tale creak, followed with a swish and click.

"Finally." Mom straightened in her seat. "I thought he'd miss dinner altogether."

The thump of footsteps travelled down the hall

toward them, but Dad didn't turn the corner to join them.

Bane, the dark fae Lord of War, strode into the Crawford's dining room unannounced and uninvited. Dressed in a business suit worth more than her car, the sleek outfit did little to hide the vicious warrior underneath.

Raven's mouth dropped open. Some mashed potatoes fell out.

Cole's eyebrows shot up and his hand froze with a fork full of roast halfway to his mouth. Not out of fear. From anticipation. The room darkened. Cole pulled the shadows to him and placed the fork on his plate.

"Well," Bane's deep voice rolled over the group. "This is cozy."

"What the fuck, dude? You don't just walk into someone's house. Haven't you heard of knocking?" Juni shrieked.

Holy balls of Odin, her sister had no idea who she just cursed at. This wasn't happening. This couldn't be happening. He was going to smite them all.

Or at least try.

"Language!" Mom snapped.

Oh no. This was happening.

"Seriously, Mom?" Mike placed his fork down on his plate and slowly reached for his steak knife. He knew who Juni had cursed at. He remembered. "A strange man just walked into our house and you're worried about swear words?"

"Well, Juni's worried about door etiquette." Raven

pointed her fork at Mike and swallowed her mouthful of potatoes. She grabbed her steak knife with her free hand, her heart thumping away. Full panic hadn't set in yet. Bane was outnumbered. They had Cole and Chloe on Team Crawford.

Mom stood frozen, clutching a kitchen knife but looking as though she'd prefer a rocket launcher. Her gaze darted to the exits. If Raven strained, she'd probably hear Mom's escape plan or smell the smoke coming off the wheels in her brain.

"And he's not a stranger," Raven continued. "Everyone, this is Bane, Lord of War. He goes by Luke Bane in the Mortal Realm."

Juni paled.

Bear scowled. "I'd prefer a stranger."

Mom didn't relax.

Oh for fuck's sake Bear, shut up. If she hadn't owed a favour to Bane to spare her twin's life, he wouldn't be sitting at this dining table at all. Raven cut a lot of deals to save her twin and she still hadn't received a thank you card. And flowers. And chocolate.

"Looks like I'm interrupting a party." Bane turned to Cole. "I see you're already attempting to mend bridges."

What did he mean by that? Was the whole Underworld following her romantic life? That wasn't embarrassing. At all.

The Lord of Shadows stood slowly and pushed back his chair. The wood creaked. More darkness pooled around him. "What are you doing here?"

The rest of Raven's family stopped bickering and stared. Oh, so that's what it took. Two dark fae lords squaring off in their dining room. Good to know.

"To speak with the Corvid Queen."

Cole flinched.

Raven frowned. Did he get hit in the head recently? Temporary amnesia? She certainly hadn't forgotten the events of that night. Gruesome images from her memory haunted her dreams. She slept horribly replaying the night she'd taken a life. She'd never killed anyone before, and she planned never to do so again. She set her fork down on her plate. The metal clanked against the smooth surface. "She's dead."

Bane turned to Cole. "You didn't tell her."

The assassin's hands curled into large fists, more shadows drew into the room and crowded the lord where he stood. His forest scent intensified.

"Of course, you didn't tell her," Bane said.

"I was going to tell her. I was giving her time," Cole said.

"For what?"

"Adjusting."

"How can she adjust if she doesn't know what she's adjusting to?" Bane snarled.

"She needed time."

"Um, hello? She's right here." Raven waved.

They turned toward her. Bane spotted the steak knife clutched in her hand and sneered.

"Tell me what?" Raven asked.

They blinked.

"What was Cole supposed to tell me?" She spoke slowly in case they needed to process her question.

The men exchanged looks—Cole's furious and Bane's smug. That probably wasn't a good thing.

Bane smirked and addressed Raven. "You're now the Corvid Queen."

Chapter Five

"I've been the queen of dysfunction and made every mistake one can make."

~*Janice Dickinson*

Bane's knowledge bomb exploded in Raven's brain. The room around her faded, the silence deafening. Her mind played back the events of that night. How she shifted into a giant raven instead of a conspiracy and chomped down on Lloth, the Corvid Queen, to prevent the power-thirsty, deranged fae leader from consuming her powers and using Bear as a battery pack.

The metallic taste of blood flooded her mouth.

Images of Lloth's broken body in a pool of blood plagued her mind. Odin's hairy nutsack, she'd killed someone. She released the steak knife and it clattered on the plate next to her fork.

Bane's words repeated over and over again.

"That's why neither of you would kill her," she whispered. Mom's world class mashed potatoes churned in her stomach.

The dark fae lords watched her with unnerving black gazes.

"I couldn't figure out why two big bad fae lords couldn't or wouldn't kill one woman when you so obviously wanted her dead." That point had always bothered her. "Now I know."

"And now you know." Bane's smug smile grew. Ugh. If she was a violent person, she'd punch that look right off his face.

Instead, she ignored him and turned to Cole. So he wasn't here to rekindle things between them. He'd planned to butter her up before sharing this crucial, life-altering information. Raven knew he kept things from her. She knew she was ignorant of the Underworld and its inner mechanisms. Yet, this felt like betrayal. "Is this why you left me the Scythe of Lloth?"

"It's called the Scythe of Corvids."

Of course it was.

"I wanted to give you more time," Cole repeated.

She nodded. She got that. He'd said it twice after all, and she wasn't dense. On top of that, she was the one who'd demanded space, and he gave it to her. She couldn't direct her anger at him. At least not realistically. Blaming Cole for her actions, or in this case inactions, would certainly be easier and might make her feel better. But no. The temporary reprieve from pointing a finger at Cole wouldn't solve her problems.

"So, wait." Mike piped up.

Raven jumped. Her awareness expanded to include the whole room. Crap. The family was still there. Her entire family, minus Dad, had witnessed the announcement. Her clothes tightened on her skin and her dark essence demanded release. The same shadowy pull that woke her in the night pulsed as if the conversation awakened it. Only Bear had known what happened that night, and now they all knew.

"Honey—" Mom reached out only to be cut off by Mike.

"Whomever kills the Corvid Queen becomes the next Corvid Queen?" Mike straightened in his chair.

Trust Mike to focus on clarifying facts instead of dwelling on his sister being a murderer.

Cole nodded. "Or king."

Well, wasn't he a big bucket of information all of a sudden?

Mike's face fell. "Does that mean others will now target my sister?"

Her whole family tensed. Raven's head snapped back. She hadn't thought of that.

Bane barked out a laugh. "Not when—"

Cole turned to him and glared.

Bane laughed harder.

Raven found zero things funny about her impending doom. She braced her hands on both sides of her dinner plate and stared daggers at Cole.

He turned to Raven. "I've extended my protection."

Everyone started speaking at once.

"What the hell does that mean?" Raven asked, not quite loud enough. She went for indignant, but her chest grew warm and her cheeks flushed with the heat. He wanted to protect her.

"Wait a damn second," Bear growled over the racket. The rest of the family let their questions trail off into silence and turned to her twin. "So, everyone in the Other Realm now thinks the new Corvid Queen is weak?"

Oh man, she hadn't even thought of that. Clearly, she wasn't the brains of the family operation.

Cole looked away.

Well, that answered Bear's question. Something she should've thought to ask herself. *Distracted by the dong again.* Luckily, Mike couldn't hear her thoughts. Her youngest brother was merciless.

"And that's incorrect, how?" Bane asked.

"Excuse me?" Bear's tone grew dangerously low.

Bane sighed and leaned over as if to speak to a five year old. "How is it incorrect for the Underworld to view your sister-dearest as a weakling when that is exactly what she is?"

Bear snarled.

"You're such an ass," Raven said.

Bane shrugged. "Yet, I speak the truth."

Cole sighed. "Most who took an interest in the events already investigated you. There's no hiding your lack of experience with the Underworld. I did what I had to do to protect you."

Cole might sugar-coat the situation, but Raven could read between the lines. Basically, she was fucked, but this option at least came with lube. "Does this job come with pay?"

"Pay?" Bane's head recoiled as if the very idea of a paycheck was foreign and offended his Other principles somehow. "Of course not."

"Then I'm not interested." She folded her arms.

"It doesn't work like that," Cole said. "You're probably already feeling the effects of the Shadow Realm."

"What does that mean?" Mom demanded.

"How are you sleeping?" Cole asked Raven.

Ice flowed along her skin. What did he know about that? Were her sleepless nights caused by more than her traumatic memories? Did he know what caused her unrest? Did he know how to stop it?

The front door slammed shut and familiar footsteps padded down the hall. Dad called out, "I'm home."

A rush of cool night air preceded Dad before he rounded the corner. Middle aged and slowing down, Dad accentuated his dad-bod with khaki pants and a polo shirt. His wiry build hinted at his wily antics as a fox shifter and the familiar sight of his brown eyes and receding hairline brought warmth to Raven's heart. "What did I miss?"

He stopped short. His gaze darted between Bane, Cole, Chloe and Bear before he turned to Raven. "I guess this is a bad time to tell you someone slashed your tires?"

Chapter Six

"Tact is the ability to tell someone to go to hell in such a way that they look forward to the trip."
$\sim$ *Winston Churchill*

Raven groaned and pushed past Bane and Dad to run to the front entrance. She'd already reached her quota for bad news. She didn't need her car vandalized. She threw the door open and hopped down the steps. She needed this car. The autumn air curled around her and the wind rustled through the remaining leaves of the trees lining the street.

Dad's spite goat lifted his head from munching grass

and bleated. After Mrs. Humphreys, the deceptively evil bigot disguised as a cute elderly neighbour, continued to call animal control regarding repeated sightings of fox in the area in an attempt to have the entire family caged, relocated or euthanized, Dad had scoured the city bylaws and discovered owning small farm pets and housing them on the property was legal. He borrowed a goat from a friend to spite Mrs. Humphreys and the poor thing had been adopted by the family.

"Hey, Pepe." Raven detoured off the path to scratch behind his ears. The goat closed his eyes and chewed on grass.

Right. Car. Slashed tires. Raven patted Pepe and cut a straight path to where she'd parked her vehicle on the street. Jean Claude Grand Am, a piece of crap well past its heyday, sat on the curb with pieces of paper the size of postcards taped to each tire.

She groaned again and slowed down. As she approached Jean Claude, the dark images on the paper grew clear. Someone had printed a figure on each piece of paper—Slash. As in the musician.

Wheezing and slapping came from behind her. She turned to find Dad laughing so hard he was red in the face, bent over and smacking his knee like the old boy at the local legion.

"Dad!"

"You should've..." He cackled. "You should've seen your face."

Bane strode down the path, gave her father a

dismissive look, frowned at Pepe and snarled at the pictures taped to the tires. He turned to focus on Raven.

Uh-oh.

"I'd like an audience with you to discuss the increasing threat of Closers," he said in a disturbingly formal tone.

"You kidnapped me and held me prisoner in a magically sealed cabin in the Underworld," she said. Why did Bane think she'd grant him anything?

Dad stopped laughing and straightened.

Yeah, Dad, you totally misjudged the situation. Again.

Dad's whole body tensed. Realistically, her fox-shifting stepdad had little chance against the Lord of War, but that wouldn't stop him from trying to protect her.

"I had a fire." Bane managed to sound offended. "It wasn't that bad."

"Yeah, real cozy."

"And plaques."

She crossed her arms over her chest and tried not to think about the odd kitschy plaques Bane had hung around his torture hut. Life was not better at the cabin, thank you very much. A gentle breeze slid over her skin, bringing hints of pine, grass and leaves, but doing little to cool the anger rising within her.

"Oh, like that jail cell Camhanaich carted you off to was so much better."

Dad's eyebrows shot up. She might've left that

detail out of her explanation of past events. Drat. They were going to have to talk after this.

"The difference is." Cole stepped from the shadows to stand between them. "I didn't keep her there."

"Well, neither did I," Bane snarled. "Technically."

Cole stepped toward the other dark fae lord. Pepe chose that moment to walk into the group and head butt Cole in the hip. The lethal Lord of Shadows looked down at the goat and frowned.

Pepe bleated.

Cole sighed and scratched behind the goat's ear. Pepe stretched his neck and strained forward for more. "Greetings, Pepe."

"She can't be coddled." Bane watched the dark fae and goat exchange with his mouth curled down. "We need her acclimatized, and fast, or the Closers will use the absence of the Corvid Queen to their advantage."

"The who?" That was the second time he'd mentioned that name. She'd never heard the term before. Did he mean the Regulators? They were a relatively harmless group of bigots who disliked any being from the Other Realms and wallowed in their own hate.

"The Corvid Queen will hear your plight in a week," Cole said.

A week? Banshee's bastard, that was barely enough time to prepare for a date. How was she to learn everything the Corvid Queen position entailed in such a short time? She still had to work, too. Bills gave zero fucks about her social calendar.

"A week!" Bane growled. "That's too much time. A lot can happen in a week."

"Exactly. She needs time to acclimatize and get up to speed," Cole said.

As much as she detested someone speaking on her behalf, she had to trust Cole spoke with her best interests in mind. What was the alternative? She had no clue what was going on. If she tried to assert her independence right now, she'd make things worse. Sometimes, it paid to keep her mouth shut.

"And in the meantime?" Bane asked.

"In the meantime, you're the Lord of War. Figure it out."

Bane narrowed his eyes. Without a word, he reached into his pocket and pulled out a disc. He threw it to the ground and a portal snapped in place. Bane turned to Raven and jabbed the air between them with his finger. "One week."

He straightened his suit jacket and stepped into the red haze. The portal snapped shut behind him, taking the disc with it and leaving the quiet fall night in the Burnaby subdivision in its place.

Raven turned to Cole.

Shadows danced in his gaze.

"Closers?" she asked.

Chapter Seven

"What feels vivid, warm, or near to you at the moment?"

~ Anais Nin

The Lord of Shadows followed Raven and padded down the stairs to her basement bedroom. She turned at the bottom to face him. Her breath caught in her chest. Full of power and muscle, he moved with the efficiency of a well-trained warrior, but the look he gave her had nothing to do with fighting.

Maybe a different F word, but definitely not fighting. Maybe she hadn't misread him after all.

Cole stepped past her, brushing her body with his own and leaving her in the wake of his intoxicating scent—the one reminding her of a mysterious forest filled with dreams and magic.

She closed the door behind them and turned to find Cole assessing her basement palace.

"This is your new room?" He turned to take in the cheesy string of lantern-style lights strung up around the crown moulding and the hastily made queen-sized bed pushed against the far wall. The Scythe of Corvids rested in the corner of the room near the bed with a dusty-rose padded bra hanging from the dull edge of the blade.

"More like old," she said. "This was my room before I moved out."

Cole ran his hands along the back of an armchair in her "sitting area." One of two, she'd saved the chairs from one of her parents' attempts to purge old furniture from the house.

"I should be thankful my dad didn't turn it into his man cave like he's threatened to do for years."

He let his hand slip from the worn leather and turned to her. Whenever he directed his full attention at her, the black in his eyes bled out and shifted like they contained their own shadows and they were delighted to see her. Or maybe she imagined all of it. Whenever she looked into his eyes though, she fell into the depths. Like a bottomless pool or a portal to an abyss or a giant tsunami swallowing her whole, she lost herself in his eyes.

"You were going to tell me about the Closers?" Oh look. She could still talk. Point for Raven.

"They're an extremist faction within the Regulators hell-bent on re-establishing the barrier between the Mortal Realm and the Other Realms," he said.

"Is that all?" She'd kind of already guessed as much.

He shook his head.

Of course not.

"They typically despise Others and supernaturals— even the ones that inhabited the Mortal Realm pre-collapse, like shifters. Closers rely on technology over magic. They have little to none of the latter and until recently, they've been nothing more than a nuisance."

"What did they do to change that assessment?"

Cole stepped closer. She backed up and her legs bumped into the other chair. If she reached out now, she could wind her hands in his shirt and pull him closer. Would he resist? Or would he welcome her touch and kiss her?

"That I cannot tell you, Einin," he said.

"Cannot or will not?"

"Get some rest. I will see you soon."

Shadows rose from the corner of the room and shrouded Cole in a whirlwind of motion. When the bands of gray faded, Cole no longer stood in front of her. She was alone in her room surrounded by only his scent.

Raven bolted upright in bed for the third, fourth or millionth time. She'd lost count. What did it matter? With a curse, she wiped the sweat from her brow and glanced at the clock. Only an hour had passed. Sleep did not come easy to her tonight and it should have. From the work hours she kept, she should be out as if someone clocked her with a sledgehammer. The chain of events and the implications kept circling in her mind, over and over again. Bane's revelations. Cole's promises. Her family's palpable fear for her safety.

Odin's desiccated nutbag, her parents had grilled her for hours. The clock may have said the "conversation" only lasted forty-five minutes, but now knowing how much she didn't know about the world, Raven wouldn't be surprised if her parents had somehow learned to bend time to extend their lectures. Who was that man? What did he mean? You killed someone? Why didn't you tell us? Why didn't Bear tell us? Who and what is a Corvid Queen? How much trouble are you in? Are we in trouble? In danger? How much can we trust this Lord of Shadows to protect us? Pack your bags, we're moving. No, don't pack your bags. Fix this, Raven. Fix this and stay alive. No, wait. Let us handle it. No...no...At this point, Mom deflated and kept swiping away angry tears while Dad wore a helpless expression and shook with rage.

"It will be okay," she'd told them, lying through her teeth as she hugged them. *I will fix this.*

How exactly she'd fix anything was beyond her, and her thoughts and fears kept attacking her brain even with her mind on the brink of blissful sleep.

A shadowy pulse of energy taunted her—the same energy teasing her every night since Lloth's death. At first, she brushed it off, assuming the feeling was another symptom of her trauma from killing the previous Corvid Queen. Like the nausea, headaches and flashbacks. But now? Maybe it had more to do with being the new Corvid Queen.

The more fatigued Raven became, the more the shadowy magic shifted and swirled inside her. This must be Lloth's power, but what could Raven do with it? How could she wield it?

The energy continued to dance and tease, shifting bands of light and shadow around the room to make her vision waver. A beacon of warmth radiated from the corner of the room. Each time she focused on the glowing scythe, the shifting stopped, and her mind settled.

She lurched from the bed and stumbled toward the Scythe of Corvids. The shadow energy spiraled and danced, churning in her stomach, creating waves in her mind. With a curse, Raven reached out and gripped the cold metal shaft of the scythe.

Everything stopped.

Silence descended.

The movement settled.

Raven closed her eyes and whimpered at the calm stillness. A tear streaked down her cheek. The coolness of the tear created a path down her flushed skin. Finally. Peace.

What now? She didn't dare let go, but she needed to sleep. She hefted the scythe off the ground and carried it with her to the bed. The bra slid off the blade. She lay down, pulled the thin sheet over her sweaty body and the scythe and blissfully closed her eyes.

Chapter Eight

"I sometimes think that God in creating man somewhat overestimated his ability."

~ *Oscar Wilde*

Raven cracked open the front door to Crawford Investigations while balancing a tray of coffee. The welcomed tang of gun oil and paper rushed over her.

Dad looked up from the front desk. He wore a blue polo shirt today and though the desk hid his pants Raven would bet money he paired the shirt with dark gray or black pants.

"You okay, Rayray?" Dad asked.

Besides having to wake up well before her usual time, her mind still reeled from last night's events. She plunked the coffee tray down on the desk and handed one to Dad—a large black coffee. Gross. "Yeah, I'm coping."

"Want to talk about it?" He repeated the same offer he made last night after she clammed up during the questioning round.

Her brain was still too scrambled and frankly, they talked enough last night. "Not yet. What's on our plate today?"

"We got a job from workers comp."

Nice. These jobs tended to be straightforward, yet, entertaining. Most people thought movies and television shows depicted private investigation accurately with the PIs acting more like bounty hunters or cops, chasing down hardened criminals in the seedy underworld. In reality, most of their work came from insurance companies or jobs farmed out by Worker's Compensation of British Columbia. At Crawford Investigations, they filled the remaining spots with cheating spouses and missing persons.

Due to her family's fox shifting abilities, which brought along an excellent sense of smell, and Raven's ability to shift into a conspiracy of ravens, which allowed her to conduct aerial and long distance surveillance without the need to carry out a rolling tail, their agency, though small, had a great reputation within the industry. The insurance company jobs were the best. They paid well and on-time, the client was detached and provided factual information, and the targets were typically low risk.

Raven returned Dad's smile. "Perfect. What's the job?"

"Teacher off on a workplace injury."

"They suspect a fraudulent claim?"

"Claims, as in plural." Dad paused. "Your friend also called."

"Megan?" Why the hell would she call here? Was she okay? What did she need?

"No."

"Oh." Raven frowned. She didn't have many friends outside her family. "Marcus?"

Dad grunted. "No. Some woman named Sarah."

The memory of Robert's fiancée with her big chestnut hair and flashing eyes popped into her head. "She's not a friend."

"Said so on the phone. Wanted the friends and family discount."

"We don't offer one of those." Not wholly true. If Megan or Marcus came to her seeking help, she'd do the job pro bono.

"That's what I told her. She's still coming in for a new client interview."

"Did you explain our rates?"

"I did. Who is she?"

"Robert's fiancée."

Dad picked up the office phone in one hand and flipped open a new folder resting on the desk's surface. He scanned the single sheet inside and punched in numbers.

"What are you doing?" Raven took a sip of her coffee. Mmm. The creamy goodness coated her tongue and warmed her belly.

"Cancelling."

Raven put her coffee down on the desk and grabbed the phone from her father.

Dad's eyes widened.

She hung up the phone. "She thinks he's cheating."

"I don't care." Dad clenched his hands. "He probably is. Not our circus, not your problem."

Raven nodded. "I know. But I want to nail his ass."

Dad opened his mouth and then shut it. He reached over, grabbed his coffee from the holder, and took a long sip.

Raven waited for him to collect his thoughts.

"Are you sure this is healthy?" he finally asked.

"Probably not, but it will feel good." She ran her fingers along the smooth surface of the desk and avoided eye contact.

Dad sighed.

"He deserves it."

"I'm not arguing that."

"Let's see what information she has and go from there."

Dad closed the file and laced his hands together on top of it. His mouth flattened and a war of emotions battled across his face. Both he and Mom struggled to take a step back from their parenting role, but at the end of the day, though Raven lived at home again, she was an adult. Technically. As Mom put it once, if Raven was old enough to make her own decisions, she was old enough to deal with the consequences, and clean up the mess.

That didn't stop Raven from seeking their advice, though, and they still tried to "help" and guide. But they identified more with free-range parenting than any helicopter parent.

Dad took another long sip of coffee. "Okay then, but promise me one thing?"

"Maybe."

"If this goes sideways...if the interview brings up too many red flags, you'll let it go?"

"Deal."

The door buzzer clicked, and Sarah sauntered in as if on cue. Wearing three-inch heels and a micro-mini too short for the occasion and the weather, and a tight revealing top, Sarah resembled a walking kid's doll. She looked good, but geez, wasn't she cold? How did she bend?

Dad stood—yup, dark gray pants. His gaze narrowed as he assessed Robert's fiancée. His nose twitched.

Yeah, she caught it, too. Sarah was some kind of shifter. Not possessing the same canny sense of smell as Dad, though, she didn't have a hint of what type.

"Hey, Sarah." Raven leaned against Dad's desk. "Any word from Robert?"

"Oh." She flipped her hair. "He's back."

Raven resisted the urge to straighten her plain T-shirt and pull up her jeans.

Dad pulled his shoulders back. "You could've called to cancel, there was no need to come all the way in."

Sarah turned to Dad and pinned him with a stern gaze. "I want to nail this fucker."

Dad's eyebrows shot up. He glanced at Raven.

She shrugged. Who was she to deny the woman vengeance? Sarah's fiancé was back from an unknown excursion, and she wanted to hire his ex to catch him, when any PI business would do. And made sure she looked hot as hell doing it, too.

Raven smiled. If it wasn't for Sarah's earlier treatment, she'd actually like this woman.

"Okay, Miss Edwards." Dad stepped forward and held out his hand. "My name is Terry Crawford. Why don't we go into the conference room and you can explain how you would like us to help you?"

The door shut, cutting off the stream of Sarah's perfume and trapping what lingered in her trail. The fuzzy, non-descript shifter scent clung to the air.

Dad turned to Raven. "That was interesting."

Her shoulders sagged. Sarah didn't provide a lot of information, but they didn't need much.

"I'll run the regular background checks," Dad said. "We'll see how much has changed since you dated him."

Raven snorted. She knew Dad investigated her

friends and past boyfriends, but this was the closest he'd ever come to admitting it.

"Let me summarize what we know," Dad said. "On July tenth, Robert didn't return home at the expected time. When he finally came home, days later, he claimed he worked a triple and slept at the hospital because he was too tired to drive. Sarah was suspicious but didn't question him further. Last Wednesday night, Robert didn't return home again. This time, Sarah went to the hospital and discovered he wasn't on shift. When he finally graced Sarah with his appearance, he gave her the same excuse." Dad flipped through his notes. "He appeared tired, had on the same clothes, wasn't clean shaven, and although he smelled of a lot of different people, that's not unusual given the nature of his job. He didn't smell like sex."

"Which is the part I find odd."

"It's all odd."

Raven drummed her fingers on her coffee cup's lid. "He's a neat freak. He presumably spent four days or so having an illicit affair. Surely, he would've showered."

Dad nodded.

"And if he didn't shower, he would've smelled like the other woman and their...activities."

Dad put his pen down. "She's a shifter, though I'm not sure which kind. Her heightened senses should've picked up sexual activity. When I asked her about his appearance, behaviour and smell she was very specific in the details."

"She wants to nail his ass. If he smelled like another woman or sex, she would've mentioned it," Raven said. Sometimes clients withheld information or lied out of embarrassment or pride, but that didn't fit Sarah. At all. That woman was out for blood and the idea of Robert getting his come-uppance made Raven practically giddy.

"So, if he's not with another woman..." Dad tapped the notepad with the butt end of the pen. "What's he doing?"

"That's what Sarah hired us to find out." Raven peered over his shoulder. "Both meetings happened in the middle of the month."

Dad handed her a calendar.

Raven set her coffee down and flipped through the pages to find the dates. "Both disappearances started on the second Wednesday of the month. This is the longest he's disappeared, though."

"What about August and September?" Dad named the two months in between the dates.

"Maybe those days fell in the middle of his shifts and he took them off to go wherever he goes without Sarah noticing. Or maybe she was out of town?"

"We'll need to confirm their schedules." Dad flipped his notepad closed. "Ask her."

Raven nodded and grabbed her coffee. "I'll arrange to go through their apartment, too."

"I could do it."

"I know, but I think I should. I know how his brain works. If I come up empty, you can do a second pass.

Besides, we have a second case."

"We do. Okay, I'll do the background checks and you confirm schedules and search their apartment. Don't wait too long."

Raven sat back in the plastic chair and cradled her near-empty coffee cup. "I'm not an amateur. He's on shift tomorrow and I'm off work. I'll go then."

"What do you think he's doing?"

Raven shrugged. "I'd say attending intensive douchebag therapy, but we both know that requires more self-awareness than Robert possesses."

"So, you have no idea what he's up to?"

"None."

"Then why are you smiling?"

"You met Sarah. We're going to find out what he's up to and she's going to take him down. This will be awesome." Maybe cosmic karma was finally kicking in.

Dad shook his head.

Uh-oh. He normally got that look when preparing to launch into a lecture about that stupid high road.

"So, what's the worker's comp case?" she asked.

Dad smirked. "WCBC believes Kelly Clementine, a grade four teacher at Capital Hill Elementary submitted a fraudulent claim."

Raven downed the rest of her coffee and set the cup down. WCBC stood for Worker's Compensation of British Columbia, a regulatory branch of the provincial government responsible for managing compensation to any employee suffering a work-related injury. A teacher submitting a fraudulent claim to the WCBC?

Raven would express surprise, but this wasn't their first teacher case. They'd investigated teachers, nurses, nuns...Delinquents came in all shapes, sizes, ethnicities, orientations, identities and occupations as Raven quickly discovered when she started working for her dad. "Kelly Clementine? Is she an online adult-content vlogger in her spare time?"

Dad looked up from the closed file in front of him. "That's a little judgmental."

She shrugged.

"Considering you go by the name Raven," Dad said.

Raven shut her mouth and glared.

Dad shrugged, imitating her to perfection. Grrr.

"What's her claim?" she asked.

"This time?" Dad flipped open the second folder and read the printout. "Back injury from taking down a display board."

"Why do they think it's fraudulent?"

"The employer lodged a complaint along with the required forms. This is Kelly's fourth claim during the same school year, and she was only back at work for a week before she mysteriously hurt herself again."

"Witnesses?"

"None."

"Camera footage?"

"In an elementary school?"

"Post collapse," she explained. After the collapse of the barrier between the Mortal Realm and the Other Realms, the world had changed.

"Good point." Dad smirked. "But no camera

footage. No one saw any of the injuries occur."

"Doctor?" Raven asked.

"She went to different walk-in clinics for each injury and saw different doctors each time."

"Loans? Debt?"

"Mike's already fishing through her finances and doing a background check. We'll know more soon."

Raven drummed her hands on the outside of her paper cup. "Paid leave?"

"She used up her paid sick leave, so now she's off on disability."

"Full pay?"

"Almost. Ninety-five percent. WCBC is compensating the employer for lost wages."

"And they're not investigating because...?" Raven asked, though she suspected the answer. It was generally the same each time.

"Backlog."

Yup, point for Raven.

"As always," Dad said.

Raven set her empty coffee cup down on the desk. "Well, we should clear this case for them pretty quickly. Seems straight forward."

"You know what they say about assuming?"

She knew what response he wanted: Assume and you make an ass out of you and me. Instead, she said, "They're premeditated disappointments?"

Dad chuckled. "I'm putting Mike on surveillance. He's setting up a cam, so we'll know when she's on the move. If you're not working at the diner, we'll need you."

Raven nodded. With her ability to shift into a conspiracy of ravens, she could follow anyone from a safe distance, undetected. Mentally making a list of all the things she needed to do for both jobs, an uncomfortable sense of unease clawed at her gut. Between these two PI jobs, and her shifts at the diner, how in Odin's wrinkled pecker would she find time to learn the fine art of badassery needed to assume the mantle of the Corvid Queen?

Chapter Nine

"Sanity is a cozy lie."

~ *Susan Sontag*

A hand reached out from an open bedroom door and wrapped around her wrist. Raven stopped and looked down at Mom's pink stiletto nails reflecting under the hallway light. The tips pressed into her skin.

"Come with me." Mom's no nonsense tone curled around her with more impact than her wrist grabbing. "Now."

"Okay..." She followed Mom into her parents' bedroom. She had to leave soon to sit on Kelly

Clementine's place, so hopefully Mom's pep talk wouldn't last too long.

Oh no. Please, don't show me the closet. She had no desire to see Dad's sociopathic wardrobe of polo shirts and identical pants.

Mom stopped by the king-sized bed covered with a gray duvet. Under the soft bedroom lighting, metal gleamed in the middle of cushioned softness.

Oooo. Shiny. Her birds perked up. At least Raven could count on one consistent thing in her life.

"What's that?" She padded closer, her feet sinking into the plush carpet.

Mom turned to her. An eyebrow arched and her lips curled. "A gun."

"I know it's a gun," Raven said. A sig P226 to be precise. "Why do you have one of Dad's guns out on the bed?"

"Well, we hardly need to worry about a toddler stumbling upon it. Besides, it's your favourite. Your dad trained you how to shoot properly and you have a restricted gun licence." She took a deep breath. "I think you should carry it with you."

"What? Why?" And holy banshee was it loaded? Mom diligently followed protocol for correct gun storage since...since forever. Apparently, gun safety went out the window. It only took some passive aggressive dark fae lords making vague threats to her safety during Sunday dinner.

Mom's hip jutted out, giving way more attitude than someone wearing tasteful fall colours and dress pants should muster. "Because the Underworld knows you now. You can't count on Cole for protection. You shouldn't. You have no official alliance and he's serving his own purpose. Besides, Crawford women stand on their own."

Somewhere, Grandma Lu cheered.

"Mom."

"Others don't do things out of the goodness of their hearts, Rayray." Elizabeth's harsh expression softened.

"I don't have a conceal to carry, or even an open carry permit for that matter. No civilian does. Not even Dad. This is Canada."

Mom snorted. "No one's paid attention to that law since the collapse. Others can die from a bullet, same as a reg."

"Mom."

"Take it." Mom picked up the gun and held it out to Raven, grip first. "It will ease my mind."

Raven stepped forward and took the firearm from Mom. Her hands curled around the familiar, cool grip. Gun oil and powder tickled her nose. Keeping her finger off the trigger, she pointed the muzzle at the corner of the room and ejected the full mag. Mom had officially lost it. "Odin's scrotum, Mom. This was loaded."

"Why wouldn't it be loaded? What good would it do you empty?"

Once Raven removed the ammunition, she observed the chamber, verified the feeding path and examined the bore. Empty.

Mom's hand wrapped around her forearm. "Others don't bluff, Raven. They don't know how. Never forget that."

Chapter Ten

"God made everything out of nothing. But the nothingness shows through."

~ Paul Valéry

Raven relaxed into the driver's seat and dropped her head back onto the headrest. "Are you sure you don't mind tagging along?"

Megan pulled another chip from the cardboard tube. "I'm just happy to be child free. I don't care what I'm doing." She tossed the chip in her mouth and closed her eyes as she chomped. The salty potato smell erupted in the small cabin area of the car and made Raven's mouth water.

Raven chuckled. Her best friend could eat a department store worth of chips if she let herself. "Yeah, but you finally get child-free time—No non-stop talking destruco-boy or squealing baby. Shouldn't you be somewhere with your feet up getting pampered?"

Megan shrugged. "I have my feet up." She wiggled her toes on the dash. "And you brought me chips, so pampering is covered as well." Her friend's brown curly hair bobbed as she nodded to herself.

"It's just not that exciting."

Megan narrowed her blue eyes. "Are you trying to get rid of me?"

"Not at all. I love company on a stakeout."

Megan smiled and popped another chip in her mouth. "I'm not even sure why we're staking out this chick if your brother already set up cams."

"That's the thing. He hasn't yet. We're staking her out manually to figure out when she's gone so we can set up the cams."

"So, why isn't Mike here?" She crunched down on another chip. Odin's scrotum she was a loud chewer. Good thing Raven parked far enough away. The sound couldn't tip off the target.

"He's still in class. He should be here in half an hour."

Kelly Clementine lived on a quiet cul-de-sac in the middle of suburbia. Her basement suite sat below a large West Coast style house that had been divided into four units to serve as an income property. The owner lived in the West End, collecting his riches in rent cheques while Kelly inhabited the bottom left unit. Streetlights cut through the inky darkness of mid-October, illuminating a path down the side of the building. Green shrubs of some kind lined the cement walkway to the target's front door.

"Ooooooo!" Megan sat up in her seat, spraying chip crumbs everywhere, and elbowed Raven in the ribs. "Look!"

Raven grunted and rubbed her side. Megan would make a terrible PI. Her overreactions would alert any nervous or paranoid target. Thankfully, Kelly appeared oblivious to her surroundings and hopefully she'd remain that way.

"I see her."

Kelly walked down the path with long, confident strides. Tight dark denim jeans accentuated her long legs and a low cut, bustier-style top emphasized her considerable cleavage. Her heels clacked against the pavement and echoed into the night.

"Doesn't look like an invalid," Megan muttered. "Or a teacher."

Raven agreed, with the first comment, at least. She tried to block all her memories from school. She held a monopod with a small video camera attached to the end and zoomed in on Kelly's face, perfectly illuminated by the overhead lights. Girl found her light, but Raven doubted she'd appreciate her glowing features when they showed the feed in court.

Kelly's cheeks held a natural healthy flush. Her lash extensions looked thick and recently applied, or she was an expert at applying the fake ones. Raven never mastered that particular skill. She always ended up with the lash glue smeared through her eye makeup. Getting extensions held a lot of appeal until Raven saw the price tag. That kind of beauty didn't come cheap.

Megan held up her binoculars and let out a low whistle. No self-respecting PI whistled in the car. Holding up the binos was bad enough. "Nice lashes."

"And nails," Raven added, watching Kelly off the camera screen.

"And hair."

Kelly Clementine didn't hurt for money, and on a reduced income, that raised a red flag all on its own. Maybe she had a sugar daddy? Or a successful side business?

Once Raven captured Kelly's face, she zoomed out to get a head to toe shot with a little extra above and below and followed Kelly as she sauntered to her car and slid into the driver's seat without a single hitch in her step.

Years ago, Mom threw her back out from tripping over one of Mike's building blocks. Not only did she demonstrate some colourful language, she hobbled for weeks. She certainly didn't strut her stuff in heels or throw herself into a car to drive off into the night.

Before Raven ditched the camera, she zoomed in and got a shot of the licence plate. Kelly maneuvered the car from the corner and the vehicle slipped into the darkness.

"Why don't you just use your phone?" Megan eyed

her set-up.

"The Canadian court system still hasn't upgraded to this century. Though the resolution is almost the same, there's an inherent distrust among jurors for videos and photos taken by a phone. Although I vehemently disagree with that, collecting evidence on my phone when and where I could've used a camera or video camera, makes me look less professional."

"That's dumb."

"Completely."

"If you have to use the video camera, why don't you use a tripod?" Megan asked.

"The monopod is still steady, and I find it more versatile. I don't have to prop it on anything."

"Huh." Megan turned to face Raven, some straggling crumbs falling from her chest. "Go time?"

Raven laughed. "No one says that."

"Well, sorry, Miss Professional PI. Not everyone has your expertise." Megan bristled. "They say it in the movies."

"I'm sorry. You're doing fine."

"Damn right I am."

Raven shook her head and placed the monopod on the backseat. She popped open the car door. The hinges of Jean Claude groaned in protest. She winced. If she had the money, she'd replace this hunk of junk. It stood out too much and made too much noise. Blending in was key to good surveillance. Luckily, she rarely conducted stakeouts or tails in cars.

With her phone on vibrate and stuffed in her jeans'

pocket, Raven walked down the street and along the path toward Kelly's door. The soft soles of her black sneakers padded on the pavement. Juni called them her B&E sneakers.

The white veneer of the target's entrance stared back at her. She knocked, not expecting an answer. Preliminary research didn't turn up any significant others, love children, friends or siblings with no respect for boundaries. If someone did answer though, Raven had an arsenal of covers.

Hearing no footsteps or the usual hollering accompanying an unexpected visit, Raven turned to the wood fence opposite of the door. She slid a small wireless spy cam from her pocket. About the size of her thumbnail, the outdoor covert tech didn't have the longest battery life, so she needed to place it so the motion detectors didn't constantly get triggered and drain the battery.

Pinching the protective cover between her fingers, she peeled back the plastic to expose the adhesive and stuck the camera low on the inside of the post where natural shadows would conceal it and the weeds from the overgrown garden wouldn't trigger the sensors with every gust of wind.

She stuffed the plastic film in her pocket. Her phone vibrated. Raven froze. She told Megan to text her if anyone pulled up to the house. Her phone vibrated again. Crap. It was one thing to talk to an unexpected guest in the house, and another entirely to run into the target. She didn't want to meet Kelly unless there was no alternative. Even with an arsenal of excuses, once Kelly saw Raven's face, Raven's chances of sneaking around unnoticed for future surveillance drastically decreased.

Raven turned to the backyard, which was separated from the walkway with a solid wood gate. The smell of cedar tickled her nose. She slipped through the entrance and quickly closed the gate, careful to lower the latch manually instead of letting it click shut.

Raven stepped into the backyard with an overgrown lawn and an unmaintained garden. She couldn't be caught in the target's fully enclosed backyard. The "I lost my cat" excuse only went so far.

The far end of the yard backed onto an alley. Raven silently groaned and jogged toward the cedar fence to gain some momentum.

She grabbed the top of the fence with both hands and hoisted her body up. She clenched her teeth and swung her legs over. Her foot caught the edge. A dog barked. Her arms screamed. With a low grunt, she threw herself over the fence and braced for impact.

Plastic and cardboard crunched. Air whooshed from her lungs. She landed on full garbage bags.

Ugh.

As thankful as she was not to land straight on pavement after vaulting a five foot fence, the ripe stench of garbage left out in the sun too long was not appreciated.

The gate by the house clicked. Had Kelly heard the racket? Did she decide to investigate? Raven froze. She couldn't move now. If she did, Kelly would hear the bags crinkle. With a silent groan, Raven kept her body relaxed against the super stuffed garbage bags. Her gag reflex pulsed. Her head rested against the haphazardly tied opening and the edge of a milk carton dug into her cheek through the thin bag. The smell of sour milk infiltrated her nose. Something wet soaked through her pant leg.

Raven continued to hold her breath to stay quiet and prevent the overpowering stench from further assaulting her nose.

After an eon or two, the gate clicked shut and the heels click clacked up the stairs toward the street. Raven let out a long breath. She rolled off the garbage bags and wiped her jeans, even though no trash actually stuck to her, and a gentle brush wouldn't be enough to get rid of the garbage juice saturating the material covering her right leg.

Something scuffed the pavement behind her. Raven whipped around and bit back a shriek. Her heart lodged in her throat and her vision swam from the fast movement.

Two large eyes glowed under the alley lights. A fat raccoon stood four feet away, patiently waiting for Raven to remove herself from the proximity of his or her dinner.

Raven eyed the garbage. Pretty stupid to leave the trash out at night. These creatures were pretty wily and ruthless when it came to getting their next meal. They could open the childproof containers that gave Raven a hard time.

The trash panda stepped forward. With a large fluffy body and a clean, healthy coat, this one didn't struggle to find food.

Raven always thought raccoons were cute, but after Dad got in a fight with one while in his fox form, Raven realized how vicious they really were. Well, everyone told her growing up they were mean, but now she knew for certain.

Dad would've lost the fight if he hadn't shifted back to a human and scared the crap out of the other animal.

The raccoon hissed. The tail puffed out. Like this one needed to look any larger.

"Okay, okay," she whispered. "I'm going."

Apparently, she had overstayed her welcome. Raven spun to go the other way and walked into a wall of muscle.

Chapter Eleven

"Instant gratification takes too long."

~ *Carrie Fisher*

Raven bounced off the hard chest and stumbled back. Strong hands reached out, gripped her arms and steadied her. Air infused with a deep magical forest caressed her skin.

Cole.

Her scalp prickled in warning. *Gee, thanks, faedar. A little late on this one.*

"Raven." His deep voice punctuated the stillness of the night. Everything else around her faded into the distance. The raccoon, the target, the potential mugger lurking around the corner. All that existed was the man standing in front of her.

"Beul na h-Oidhche gu Camhanaich," she whispered.

His hands tightened on her arms briefly before falling away.

Did her presence affect him in the same way? Did her voice conjure images of their time together?

Cole wrinkled his nose. "I prefer when you smell of the rain."

Awareness of her surroundings crashed back. The garbage. The smell. The giant dark fae lord in an alley. Oh crap.

She would've preferred to smell like anything other than soiled trash, but the world always conspired against her.

A small smile cracked Cole's serious expression. His teeth shone under the streetlights, while his porcelain skin glowed. The rest of him was mired in darkness— jet black hair and clothing made him all but disappear.

"Why are you here?" she asked.

"Can't a man admire the finesse and grace of an expert fence vaulter?"

She snarled.

"I particularly enjoyed how you stuck the landing."

"Now you're just being mean." She folded her arms. "Why are you really here?"

"It's time for your crash course on the Queen of Corvids and Underworld courts." He stepped forward, undoubtedly to gather her in his arms again and whisk her off to the Other Realms.

"Um...no!" She jerked back and stopped him with a hand on his chest. His heart beat slow and steady under her palm.

His dark brows pinched in.

"My friend is waiting for me."

"The one in your car?"

She narrowed her eyes. Exactly how long was he watching her? "Yes."

"Text her later." He reached forward.

Raven slipped from his grip and danced backward on her tiptoes. "I can't text her later. There's no reception in the Underworld. She'll think something happened to me and call in the cavalry."

"The cops?" Cole sneered.

Well, okay, snob. Apparently, the VPD didn't have any street cred with the patron fae of assassins.

"No." She unfolded her arms and placed her hands on her hips. "My mother."

Cole paled. Though his interactions with her mom were limited, and positive, Cole still picked up on the crazy simmering beneath the tanned surface of Elizabeth Crawford's skin.

"Text her now. I'll wait."

"Hang on." Raven pulled out her phone and texted Cole instead of Megan.

His pocket buzzed and he pulled out his phone from his dark jeans. He read the screen, his gaze snapping back and forth while he held perfectly still. His eyebrows shot up. "No?"

She winked and spun on her heel. The raccoon hissed at her again, this time with a partially eaten chicken leg clutched in its paw.

Cole didn't reply, but the shadows pulled around her and brushed her skin before flowing down the alley. Just like that—gone.

Her feet slapped the pavement as she walked around the block and made her way back to the car. The cool air pushed against her skin, making her eyes water a little. Megan waited inside, vibrating with eyes the size of Mom's favourite display dish. If Raven paused long enough, she'd probably hear all the questions tumbling around in her friend's brain. Luckily, Megan waited to voice them until Raven slipped into Jean Claude and shut the door.

"How'd it go? Did you plant the spy cam? Did Kelly see you?" She paused to brush the chip crumbs stuck to her sweater off her chest. "Did you get busted? How'd you get away? Why do you smell like garbage?"

Raven sighed and turned the key in the ignition. Her car's engine sputtered to life. "It's a good thing we have a long drive home."

Megan's face scrunched up. "I'm not so sure lucky is the right word. Ugh. The smell is getting worse."

Raven laughed and pulled the car away from the curb. Her stomach twisted as she recounted the events to her friend. She enjoyed sharing the details with Megan and laughing away the tension knotting her shoulders and neck, but a cloud always loomed over her when she shared information with Megan. And the cloud just got bigger and bigger, darker and darker.

Raven left out any mention of Cole and the dark courts of the Underworld. She'd lied to her friend for years. Sure, it was by omission, but if the truth ever came out, if she ever owned up to it, Megan wouldn't see the distinction.

For their entire friendship, she'd let Megan believe she shifted into a fox like the rest of her family. Mom's incessant nagging and warnings had prevented her from sharing the truth regarding her mixed heritage with Megan when they were younger, but now, as adults, she'd maintained the lie. Guilt plagued and weighed down her soul.

Maybe she should just tell her. The longer she perpetuated the lie, the harder it would be to come clean. A memory surfaced and Raven slammed the lid on that possibility. About a month ago, she'd found pamphlets supporting Regulators in Megan's house and her friend parroted some of the common arguments against the Others. If her best, and only, friend discovered Raven was *one of them*, the evil dark fae she needed to protect her kids from, would she still want Raven as a friend? Could Raven recuperate emotionally if Megan's hatred for Others proved stronger than her love for Raven? Could Megan forgive Raven for the years of deceit?

Raven didn't have any answers and she was too chickenshit to find out.

Chapter Twelve

"You can get the monkey off your back, but the circus never leaves town."

~ *Anne Lamott*

Raven braced as the door to her ex's sin bin swung open to reveal an impatient fiancée on the other side.

"I don't know why you insisted on searching our place," Sarah said. "I've already looked everywhere." She'd plaited her chestnut hair today and wore ripped jeans and a plaid shirt. She'd left one too many buttons undone to show off her ample cleavage.

Raven took a deep breath and pulled her shoulders

back. "It always helps to have a neutral third party take a look." *And you know, a professional.* But the last thing Raven needed right now was a pissing match with her client.

"Except, you're not exactly neutral, are you?" Sarah stepped back and waved Raven in with her manicured claws. Seriously, how did anyone function with fake nails that long?

"If you had a problem with that, you shouldn't have hired me." Raven stepped into the house and took in a deep breath of fresh linen scented air. "To be honest, I thought my past with Robert was an endorsing factor."

A wicked grin spread across Sarah's face, flashing obnoxiously perfect teeth.

Yeah, Raven wouldn't cross this woman anytime soon. Robert had messed with the wrong person. Finally.

"Where do you want to start?" Sarah asked.

"His office." Robert was a creature of habit. He treated his office as a man cave and when they were together, Raven found evidence of his infidelity amongst his research papers for university.

Sarah nodded and closed the door behind Raven. "This way."

Sarah walked down the hall and opened the first door on the left. Raven walked past her and straight into a sterile room with a small window overlooking the courtyard outside.

Einstein once asked, "If a cluttered desk is a sign of a cluttered mind, what is a clear desk a sign of?" Or something along those lines. If Robert was any indication for the answer to that particular question—a narcissistic douchebag.

Raven paused.

No. That label was too kind, but Raven needed to clear her mind and push her biases to the side. She had a job to do.

Raven needed to find something incriminating or any hint of what Robert was up to on the days in question. She turned to Sarah. "Where were you on August fourteenth and September eleventh?"

Sarah recoiled as if Raven had physically slapped her. If only. "Excuse me? This isn't about me. I'm not on trial."

"No. But we want to establish whether Robert's absences have a pattern or rule out the possibility of a pattern. Can you check?"

Sarah rolled her eyes and dug out the phone in her bra. Her long nails clicked against the screen as she tapped the pad of her forefinger on the screen. "August fourteenth and September what?"

"Eleventh."

Sarah scrunched her lips together and flicked through her calendar. "I was out of town August twelfth to September thirteenth. When I came back, Robert took me to that shitty diner you work at."

Raven bit her tongue and ignored the bird energy coiled inside her. Sarah wasn't wrong. The diner sucked. Saying so to Raven's face, however, was rude and most likely meant to hurt her feelings. Raven pushed the comment to the side to sit on the bench with her biases and focused on the important stuff. What did Mike say Sarah did for work again? Corporate programmer? "That's a long trip."

Sarah shrugged. "We set up a new call center overseas and I oversaw the operation."

Fair enough. Raven turned to Robert's desk. She flipped open her ex's laptop and started it. "Any chance you know the password?"

Sarah snorted somewhere behind her. Of course, she did.

Raven stepped to the side and let the other woman log on. Once again, a slightly furry scent prickled her nose. Definitely a shifter, but not a fox. Too bad Dad hadn't placed it with his nose or turned up the information on his background check. Why would Sarah hide it? Only a few shifter types hid their nature from other shifters.

"Here you go." Sarah stood back and stared at the computer as if it housed her worst enemy. In a way, if it held information about Robert's cheating, it kind of did.

"Thanks." Raven pulled her phone out and called Mike.

"Sup?" Mike's muffled voice answered on the third ring.

"I'm on his computer," she said.

"Okay, hold on," Mike mumbled.

"Are you eating? Again?" Of course, he was eating. By the end of the day, Mom resorted to chucking whatever food was left in the pantry at him. They went through a lot of bread and cereal, so much so, Raven wouldn't be surprised if he started sprouting wheat for hair. Her nineteen-year-old brother was a bottomless pit surpassed only by Juni, constantly filled with simple carbohydrates and processed food without any negative impact to his hips, thighs or ass.

Life wasn't fair.

She only asked the question because she specifically told him her plans and he was supposed to be ready.

"Of course, I'm eating," he said. A door creaked on his side of the line. He must've entered his room, aka the battle station. "It's just a snack."

Raven rolled her eyes and navigated the computer's system to find the information she needed.

"Okay, I'm ready," Mike said.

Raven prattled off the IP address and watched the mouse icon move on its own after Mike remotely hacked into her ex's computer.

"Got it. I'll clone it now and go through the files later." He hung up without a goodbye.

"Sounds good," Raven spoke to her phone screen. She stuffed the device back in her pocket and straightened.

Sarah leaned against the door frame with folded arms and a curled lip. Her jeans hugged every curve like a second skin. Apparently, the fiancée wanted to supervise.

Whatever. Raven spent the next forty minutes searching the office and the rest of the apartment.

"See?" Sarah said as she shuffled behind her, the

soft carpet absorbing the impact and sound of her sock-covered feet. "I told you there was nothing."

Raven bit her tongue and pulled the rubber gloves from her back pocket. She always saved this part for last. The plastic squeaked as she stretched the gloves over her hand.

Sarah's eyebrows shot up.

"Garbage," Raven explained. She pivoted and headed back to the office. No self-respecting PI neglected the garbage when conducting a search. One man's trash was a PI's much needed lead.

Unfortunately, it appeared Raven would end up with nothing but Sarah's attitude.

Her phone buzzed while she flipped through receipts. She snapped one glove off and pulled her phone from her pocket to read the message. Mike had texted, "Done."

Raven turned to Sarah while stuffing the phone in her jeans again. "You can log out of the computer now and turn it off."

Normally, it didn't take forty minutes to clone a laptop. At least not for Mike. Having that stinky cast hadn't slowed him down much, either. If he took a break to refuel, she'd kill him. Or at least have a stern conversation with her baby brother about responsibility, accountability and professionalism.

"This has been a complete waste of time." Sarah sauntered over to the laptop and shut it down.

Raven scrunched up her face and resisted the urge to point out how Sarah didn't have to accompany her to every room. Instead, she glanced at the last of the receipts still clutched in her one hand. She wiggled her hand back in the glove and unfolded the receipts to scan their information.

Hang on.

October ninth. The date Robert went missing. He must've emptied his pockets in the office trash. Idiot.

Luckily, the dumbasses of society kept Crawford Investigations in business.

She rifled through the last of the garbage and found one more receipt for the same date range. She recognized the popular downtown café. He'd ordered a latté and a pumpkin spice scone. She stuffed the rest of the contents back in the garbage bin and pushed it back in place.

Maybe not so emptyhanded after all. She folded the receipts and slipped them into her back pocket. She pulled off one glove, held it in her palm and peeled off the other glove so it folded over the first one. She shoved the wad of latex into her other back pocket. Robert's trash was all paper, so she wasn't worried about germs. She was, on the other hand, concerned with his complete disregard for their already failing environment. Had he never heard of recycling?

"I'm done here," Raven said and straightened from her squatting position. Her muscles complained.

"What did you find?"

"Hopefully, a lead. I'll let you know when I have something solid."

"I want to know now." Sarah flashed her teeth.

"No."

"No?" Sarah's whole body stiffened as if she never heard the word before.

"No." Raven was getting some solid practice at using that word lately. Grandma Lu would be so proud.

"Why not?" Sarah's hands clamped onto her hips.

"Because I can't have my vigilante client storming off to investigate my leads and potentially destroying or tampering with evidence, or unnecessarily tipping off the target." The receipts burned in her pocket.

"You're my employee and I'm not planning to take Robert to court. Maintaining the integrity of evidence isn't a requirement of your job."

The shifting dark energy in Raven's core pulsed. As if it had a mind of its own and took offence to Sarah's tone, the power pushed at her skin from the inside. The force of motion so strong, it threatened to break Raven at the seams. Her hands itched to reach for the power and grab...something. What did the corvid energy call for? What did it want?

Raven grit her teeth and forced her breathing to remain steady, though her heart raced like a horse at a derby. "Yes, and you signed a contract. Let me do my job and I'll get you the information. You need to trust me, take a step back from all of this and not interfere."

Sarah's face contorted as if Raven fed her a lemon instead of the truth. "Do you need anything else?" she finally bit out.

"Yes."

Her client scowled.

The pulse of dark energy eased away. "Do you share the same account for your phone's app store and music?"

Sarah pursed her lips. "How did you know?"

Robert was a creature of habit. Raven would bet her last pair of non-discount bin pants Sarah had her name and credit card information on the account, too. "Your fiancé likes to pinch his pennies."

Sarah snorted. "That's not what's going to get pinched when I bust him."

They shared a smile and warmth spread through Raven's chest. Oh, she sincerely hoped Sarah spoke the truth. "I need your phone."

Sarah pulled the device out from somewhere in her bra and handed over one of the newest models on the market in a glittery, bedazzled case. It was still warm. Ew.

Raven quickly navigated through the app store and found the program to download. Originally intended to retrieve a lost device on the same account, not stalking a loved one, the app had come in handy in previous cases. Conveniently, it didn't require consent or acknowledgement from the other device user, unlike the popular friend finding app. She handed the phone back to its owner.

"What is this?" Sarah stared at the phone screen and the downloading app.

"If we don't figure out what happened by the time he goes missing again, you're going to call me and we're going to use this app to track him."

Sarah stared at her phone screen and the creepy evil smile spread across her face.

All right, then.

Raven should feel sorry for Robert and the eventual misery this woman planned to put him through, except, well, she didn't. She wasn't a big enough person for that kind of compassion and forgiveness. Robert deserved every piece of revenge coming his way.

Chapter Thirteen

"There's only one basic principle of self-defence—you must apply the most effective weapon, as soon as possible, to the most vulnerable target."

~ Bruce Lee

Raven stepped from Sarah and Robert's house and inhaled autumn air, fresher in this neighbourhood than the one she lived in and filled with dry leaves and sweet pine needles. Her phone vibrated in her pocket again. She yanked it from her jeans and accepted the call from Dad.

"Hey!" she said.

"Hey, Rayray. I finished running through Robert's

background check." He sounded tired.

"Anything?" She looked both ways and crossed the street. Her sneakers slapped the dry pavement and crunched random dirt littering the road. She'd parked a few blocks away because Jean Claude wasn't exactly inconspicuous, and she couldn't assume Robert didn't have loyal friends. She might be a random girlfriend visiting his fiancée while he worked, but if a nosy neighbour was also able to describe her car, the gig was up.

"Nothing overtly suspicious. He refinanced the mortgage on the house six months ago, but a lot of people do that."

"Any access to his finances?" She referred to the private, personal records.

A long pause. "You know that's against the rules."

Raven sighed. Yes, she knew that, just as she knew Dad would never cross that line. Why had she even asked? Dad represented everything good in the world. He wouldn't break the law unless it was to protect his family.

But she knew who would. Mental note: call Bear.

"Have you run Sarah a second time, yet?" she asked.

"No, it wasn't a priority. I was focusing on our other case. Why?"

"Just a vibe I get from her." She stepped through a pile of dry leaves. *Crunch. Crunch. Crunch.*

Dad chuckled, low and rumbly. "Well, she's a shifter and engaged to Robert."

"Yeah, I picked up a little fuzz in her scent." She

took the high road and didn't comment on Robert. "But there's something off about her. Something sinister."

"What are you thinking?"

Raven turned another corner. A cool breeze washed over her. "Not sure yet. She's hiding her nature and she wears socks in the house, so she doesn't shift a lot. Maybe jackal or raccoon." Just the two biggest shifter-run gangs in the Lower Mainland known for less than legal business dealings with the Other Realms. No big deal.

"Normally, I'd pick up either of those scents. She must wear a scent-cloaking spell of some kind." Dad grunted. "I'll look into it."

"Okay, I'll—"

A large hand grabbed her arm and hauled her into the alley. Another hand clamped over her mouth and muffled her cry. The man's skin smelled like smoke and oil. She flailed, her arm flung out and sent her phone flying.

"Raven?" Dad's voice barked on the other side of the line as the phone flew through the air. "RAVE—"

The phone smashed against the pavement near the entrance of the alley with a loud crack.

Raven flinched.

The man pulled her back, his beefy arm holding her across her body, pinning one arm against her side while he gripped the other with his hand.

His Other energy vibrated along her skin, soaked into her essence and dampened her own power, like a soggy towel. A shiver crept along her spine and her hair coiled into tight curls around her face.

His other hand still covered her mouth.

"If you scream, I will hurt you. Do you understand?" A deep voice fanned her ear. Not Cole's. Not Bane's. Great. Like she needed another dangerous man in her life.

Raven gulped and nodded. The hand slipped from her mouth. Was that even smart? Maybe she should've let him keep it there so she could bite him, draw blood and summon Cole.

"She's going to get hurt anyway." Another voice drew Raven's attention.

A tall, lean man with dark hair, gray skin and the all-black eyes of the Other Realms turned the corner and walked into the alley toward them. His boots clicked on the pavement. His face had all the right components to make him handsome, but something about their sharpness and the calculation of his gaze gave him too harsh an appearance for that word.

"I don't have any money." She didn't even need to lie about that.

The man's thin lips widened to show jagged teeth. Like a shark. "I'm not here to rob you, *Bhanrigh*."

Raven narrowed her eyes. She reached for her raven energy, but the other man still held her wrist and his power muted hers. Odin's nutsack, she was getting sick of this. For some reason, dark fae energy short-circuited her own and she didn't know why. What she did know was she always struggled to access her abilities when someone from the Other Realms physically touched her.

Except Cole.

Warmth bloomed in her chest at the thought of the Lord of Shadows, despite the serious situation. When Cole touched her, the dark powers she harboured inside came to life.

Well, Cole wasn't here to help her. And neither were her powers, apparently. Even the shifting energy faded from her awareness. Time to flex that good ol' noggin.

She pushed her hand down and fumbled with her shoulder bag clasp. Mom was right about many things, including the vulnerability of Others to bullets. If only she could reach the gun.

"What do you want?" she hissed.

The man smirked. Totally corny evil 90s henchman style, but that didn't make him any less dangerous. A shark. That was it. He reminded her of a shark. "I want to work with you."

"Terrible way to start a business relationship." The words sounded familiar. Hadn't she said something similar to Luke Bane when he kidnapped her? And what in the Underworld? She was getting nabbed off the street faster than discount chocolate after Valentine's Day. She needed to level up her defence.

Shark Man shrugged while her other captor, the Muscle, tightened his grip.

"There's no need for charades, Bhanrigh. You will have little choice but to do as I say once I get you back to my realm." He shifted a little to the side, crunching leaves as he moved.

"Why on earth would you want me as a minion?" Raven couldn't even get out of this hot mess. What about her made Shark Man think she was up for any menial task?

"You're the Corvid Queen."

"Then just kill me, already and take my job." Wait...what? Raven cringed. What in Odin's shriveled beanstalk was wrong with her? That was probably the most fundamentally stupid thing she'd ever said. And she wasn't a stranger to stupid.

The Muscle's chest vibrated against her back and a deep chuckle rumbled past her ears.

Shark Man laughed. His jagged teeth gleaming. "You really are as clueless as they say. Only someone with corvid essence can assume the mantle. If you're killed by someone without the right pedigree, the power and responsibilities of the Shadow Court will transfer to Camhanaich. No one wants that, least of all the Lord of Shadows."

What. The. Fuck. Once again, Cole left out an important tidbit. Why? Unimportant? Just forgot? Self-serving? Wanted to trickle feed her information in fear her brain might overload and combust?

And, more importantly, did she care? Did this omission hurt her in some way? Would having this information in advance change the sequence of events that led to now? Not really. No matter how she sliced it, she'd end up here...screwed.

Raven had no idea how to feel about any of this. But

she did know her feelings wouldn't matter at all if she didn't survive the current situation. She squirmed and pushed her arm into her bag. *Say something else. Anything.* Keep distracting this guy from taking her away from the alley. "So, you plan to haul me to your domain and torture me into doing your bidding?"

Shark man sighed, a long, pained release of air. "They said clueless. They didn't say dense, as well."

Raven drove her heel into her captor's knee. He grunted. She raked his shin and stomped hard on his foot. He howled and his grip loosened. Her heartbeat pounded in her ears. She drove her arms up and dropped her body down, out of the grip of the Muscle. He clutched the air where she'd stood. Before he could regain control, she grabbed his arms and used his own lurching forward momentum to throw him toward Shark Man. She ducked behind him as he flew past and scrambled to her feet. Thank you, self-defence class.

The man stumbled a few feet ahead but regained his footing.

Well, damn.

Raven's heart thudded. She fumbled with the flap of her bag. She needed to get the gun. She chucked contents out of the way as she frantically dug through the bag. Keys, nope. Wallet, nope. Pens, nope. Old pack of gum, nope. The items clattered to the pavement.

Wait.

She could just shift away.

A loaded gun sat in her purse where anyone, including a child, could find it. Leaving it here would be irresponsible. She glanced at her wallet. Her licence was in there. She had her family's home address on it. If they tracked her here, though, surely they could—

Growling interrupted her racing thoughts. Both men, one thin and gray, the other muscle-bound and golden with a surprisingly handsome face, gnashed jagged teeth and trained their dark Other gazes at her.

Shark Man pulled out some sort of tube and held it to his mouth.

"No!" Raven brought her arms up and pulled hard at her raven essence.

Not fast enough.

Before the dark energy could spiral up and rip her consciousness into a conspiracy of ravens, a red dart embedded into her forearm. Pain bloomed at the point of contact. Instantly, a film of gray coated her Other essence and soaked in, smothering her ravens. She wobbled. The edges of her vision closed in and she staggered. Her back hit the cold surface of a building and she slid down until she slumped on the dirty pavement. The ground smelled of dirt and decay. Cool air brushed past her numb cheek.

Silver streaked through the air, reflecting sunlight— bright flashes sparkling in her gray vision. Daggers sank into the chests of both men. Their eyes widened. They glanced at each other, before they fell to the ground with loud thumps.

Shark Man's vicious face landed a few inches from

her foot, his once-calculating gaze now blank.

The gray film continued to spread through her mind and cloud her visions. Her eyelids grew heavy. She lowered to the ground and lay on her back. The blue sky above lost its vibrant colour as the world around her closed in. Her heart slowed. Her breathing grew shallow.

A man stepped over her and peered down, his bulk blocking out the last of the light. Shadows obscured his face but not the long dagger he held perilously close to her body. His other hand reached up to his ear. Did he have a phone? An earpiece? Her vision wavered and continued to close off.

"Camhanaich," the man said, his voice low and growly. "We have a problem."

Chapter Fourteen

"Tact is the art of making a point without making an enemy."

$\sim$ *Sir Isaac Newton*

The fog lifted from Raven's brain. She opened her eyes to a familiar room and brushed tightly coiled black hair from her face. She knew this soft, natural light and cedar-plank ceiling. She saw the room in her dreams every night. If she closed her eyes, she'd recall each plank and the iron-wrought chandelier hanging from the center of the ceiling to light the large bedroom. Then the memories would return with acute vividness of how a man had pinned her to this bed and how she'd lost herself to the sensations he evoked as he broke her world apart and put it back together again, and again, and again with the rhythm of his body. And then, her chest would ache from the loss.

She kept her eyes open and willed the memories to leave her alone.

Dark otherworld energy ran along her skin and pulled at her power. Like a rambunctious four year old, it beckoned for her to come play.

Cole's bedroom in the Shadow Realm. Orange sunlight poured through the small spaces between closed slatted blinds and bathed the room in natural light. The whole place smelled of him. She sank back into the plush pillow, the bedding cocooned her in warmth against the cool air. She was safe. Those two men were probably just the beginning of a long line of fae intent on her downfall, but Cole wouldn't let anything happen to her. Those same two men were now dead.

Dead.

A shadow traveled over her clothed body. Not a shadow moving with the changing position of the sun. And certainly not a living shadow like the ones Cole controlled and used to tease her senses and kill thugs alike. A regular shadow.

She wasn't alone.

She turned to the side. A menacing Other stood two feet from her in Cole's bedroom. Not Cole. She'd met this one before—a weapon warper with deadly aim and poisoned daggers. Raven scrambled to sit up.

The man held up his hands. Empty. No weapons. But that meant nothing. He was the star of some of her nightmares. He'd thrown a dagger at her head, and had she not been cloaked in Cole's shadows, he would've killed her.

He opened his mouth, showing off his jagged teeth.

For fuck's sake was this a new fashion trend?

"You," she said. The assassin had taken the job issued by the guild with two comrades. He was the only survivor. After Cole spared his life, he sent Raven's would-be-killer back to the guild to pull the hit on her life.

"My name is Rourke, but if you wish to call me 'you,' that is permitted."

"You threw a dagger at my head." She tapped her temple with her forefinger, in case he needed a reminder.

The man's grin broadened, and he lowered his I-surrender arms. "And now I belong to the Lord of Shadows."

"If it's such a penalty, why are you smiling?"

"There are worse fates for mistakes in the Underworld. Belonging to Camhanaich isn't that bad." He leaned into the wall and folded his arms. "But I don't need to tell you that, do I?"

Her head snapped back. A wave of nausea spread through her body. "I don't belong to Cole."

Rourke raised his eyebrows. "He has plenty of spare bedrooms, yet, here you are."

"I don't belong to him."

"Have you told him that?"

She scowled.

"I don't imagine it would do much good, even if you did." He continued to smile with jagged teeth.

"What do you mean by that?" She dug her hands into the soft bedding and resisted the urge to pull the plush comforter around her. She belonged to herself, thank you very much.

Rourke pushed off the wall and stepped toward the bed.

Raven flinched.

Rourke stopped walking immediately and frowned.

"You're scary."

Rourke's wide grin returned, pointy teeth and all. "Good. Maybe those idiots will think twice before trying to harm or kidnap you again."

Again? Those two weren't going to try anything ever again. How many other idiots did she have to worry about? Besides herself. She pulled the sheets back and swung her legs over to the side of the bed. Her head swam.

"Careful. The toxin is still working its way through you."

"Poison?"

"In a sense. It's a toxin found in the Sefton beetle of the Underworld. It temporarily neutralizes Other energy."

"What's a Sefton beetle?"

"I guess you could say it's the Underworld's

equivalent of a dung beetle."

Ew. Gross. She planted her hands on the edge of the bed to steady herself. "They injected me with toxin from a poop beetle?"

"Worse." Rourke shifted the weight on his feet and looked away.

Oh great. The information made the big bad metal-warping assassin uncomfortable.

"The toxin actually comes from their excrement."

Wait a minute. "They pumped me full of poop from a poop beetle?"

"Pretty much."

Her skin crawled.

"The men dosed you as a full-blooded Other, probably not willing to risk you'd shake it off if they diluted it too much. We don't know if the amount they gave you will cause any adverse reactions, yet, due to your half blood."

Raven shuddered. How many people knew her origin story? How much did these Others gossip? She'd barely come to terms with having Odin's creations as her biological fathers, but apparently, now it was common knowledge. "You seem to know a lot about me."

Rourke cocked his head to the side like an amused cat. Not a housecat, something larger and more lethal. "The whole Underworld does."

"Cole?"

Rourke laughed and the sound echoed in the large room. "Camhanaich wouldn't confess on his deathbed."

"Then who?"

"Your grandsire is very proud."

She groaned and flopped back in the bed. Wasn't information supposed to be power? Why would Odin provide information about her? Now she'd inherit his enemies along with his...

Oh.

"Everyone knows Odin is my grandfather," she said. "They'll risk his wrath along with Cole's."

Rourke nodded. "He must've figured the benefit of revealing his connection to you outweighed the risks. He cares enough that he'd destroy anyone who harmed you, but not enough for you to be used against him."

"Gee, thanks."

"It's a good thing he did what he did. You need protection." His gaze assessed her without heat. He pursed his lips. "You're incredibly weak."

"Hey!"

Rourke shrugged. "Avoiding the truth won't change it."

"Is there some sort of accelerated learning program for noobs?"

"I'm not sure what a noob is, but why don't we start with getting you a shower?" His nose crinkled.

"That's enough." Cole's unexpected voice growled from somewhere behind her.

She spun in the bed, rustling the sheets around her.

Cole walked from a tangle of shadows. "I'll take it from here."

"Of course." Rourke smirked and bowed. When he straightened, he winked at Raven and walked with silent footsteps toward the door. For a guy who'd previously tried to kill her, he didn't seem so bad.

What the hell was in that toxin?

"Rourke," Cole voiced a name and a command at the same time.

The weapon warper stopped and turned to face the Lord of Shadows.

"Thank you for keeping her safe."

Oops. Guess she should've thought of that. Lifesaving wasn't covered in etiquette class—not that Raven ever attended one of those—but she didn't need any instruction to know Rourke's actions deserved a heartfelt apology. And saying one now would come across as a hollow echo of Cole's words.

"See Niall on your way out," Cole said.

Who? Did other people live here? Raven's cheeks heated. How good was the sound-proofing?

Rourke bowed again and left the room, shutting the door behind him. The loud click initiated deafening silence. The room shrank the moment he left her alone with her thoughts and Cole.

The dark fae lord turned to her, his eyes blazing with swirls of black. His gaze raked her body and his expression darkened. "Enough of this, Raven. You can't avoid the Underworld. You need the essentials. Not someday. Not later. Now."

She sighed. She didn't conveniently have Megan sitting in her car and waiting for her as an excuse to avoid this particular *pleasantry* this time. But even she wasn't dumb enough to ignore the importance and necessity of getting help. "I need to call home. I was on the phone with my dad when they attacked me. They're probably freaking out right now."

"I already contacted your family. They know you're safe and the threat's been neutralized. And as you've already pointed out, electronic devices don't work in the Underworld."

"I'd still like my phone."

Cole tugged something out of his pocket. He tossed the mangled remains of the phone onto the bed. It smacked a pillow, slid down beside her and sank into the bedding. "I'll get you a new one."

"No, you won't." She eyed her old phone and mentally cursed. She needed a new one.

Cole smiled.

"I'm serious."

"Do you have some spare money kicking around to buy yourself a new one?"

If she glared hard enough, maybe he'd feel the daggers and she'd inflict actual damage.

"Consider it a 'Welcome to the Underworld' gift."

"Did you just make a joke?"

"Maybe?"

"You sound unsure."

"You didn't laugh."

"Ha, ha."

Cole's jaw clenched. "Cute."

Maybe taking lessons from the Lord of Shadows

wouldn't be so bad if she could pass the time mocking him. Instead of withering in her hot need to touch his body, she'd endure his survival lessons without making a complete ass of herself.

Shadows pooled around Cole, sliding up her body and surrounding her on the bed. He wore them like a cloak or shield, and all she thought about was ripping them away with her teeth. Survive his lessons? Probably not. "So...uh...as much as I appreciate the welcome gift and the offer for free tutoring, I still have bills to pay. You've pointed out my lack of funds, yourself."

Cole walked around the bed to where she sat. "Who said I offered my tutoring for free?"

She folded her arms. "I'm not paying."

He crouched down until he was eye level with her. "Oh, but, Einin. You haven't asked the price, yet."

She shook her head. If she'd been born an ostrich, she'd happily shove her head in some sand right now. "No deal."

His grin grew and he leaned forward. It took every ounce of self-control not to scramble away or launch herself onto his body.

"The training will be rigorous." His deep voice rumbled over her skin. "Surely, I deserve some compensation."

"I'm not a prostitute."

Cole recoiled. "That's not what I was suggesting."

She rose her eyebrow. "So, you weren't suggesting I have sex with you in exchange for your help?"

He clamped his mouth shut and shook his head. After a deep breath, he spoke. "That's not how I meant it."

Inherently, she knew he didn't, but she needed an excuse to remove herself from this situation before she threw herself at him. She shimmied across the bed and flung her legs over the side before Cole could block her with his freakishly strong body. "I need to go to work."

"You need to learn, Einin." He moved so fast she couldn't track it. One moment he was beside her and the next he appeared right in front of her. A hand braced against the mattress on each side of her hips, trapping her in a sitting position on the bed while he hovered, half crouched in front of her. He looked ready to pounce. Like a big cat. A big, deadly, sexy cat.

"I'm not sleeping with you for information."

"First, there would be little sleeping," Cole growled. "And second, I'm not demanding payment of any kind and you know it. I will tutor you, and you will learn."

"Fine," she said. "But I need to work."

Cole grumbled. "Fine."

"Will you take me back?"

"Will you swear an oath to attend training if I schedule them around your two jobs?"

"Yes," she bit out.

"Then, yes."

She waited.

He stood and held his hand out. She slipped her hand into his larger one, skin sliding against rough callouses, and let him haul her off the bed. His arms wrapped around her, but the shadows didn't carry them off to the Mortal Realm.

"Um..." She looked up at Cole.

He stared back at her expectantly. "Aren't you forgetting something?"

Understanding swept through her body in a hot wave of anticipation. The last time they'd made a deal, Cole had sealed it with a mind-altering kiss. Surely, he didn't mean... "Is there another way to seal the deal?"

Another grin spread across his face. "I can think of many ways."

Raven rolled her eyes and reached up to grip each side of his face. "I, Raven Crawford, swear to attend your training sessions if you schedule them around my work."

Cole leaned down and whispered something in fae. At this point, she didn't care if he recited his mother's coveted fruitcake recipe. Cole's mouth met hers and all thoughts of self-preservation flew out the window. His lips pressed against hers, sin and dark promises wrapped together. She melted into his arms and dark fae magic curled around them, sealing the promise of their deal while whispering against her skin.

The shadows rose up and carried them away.

Chapter Fifteen

"I only go out to get me a fresh appetite for being alone."
~ Lord Byron

R aven watched Kelly Clementine enter the café on Richards through the eyes of her conspiracy. The same café Robert had a receipt for. Raven would be suspicious of the coincidence except this was one of the most popular downtown Vancouver cafés.

Though Cole stressed the necessity of training, he'd let her escape to the Mortal Realm to work on the promise she'd adhere to his proposed training schedule. Her lips still tingled from the oath sealing kiss. If she closed her eyes, she'd taste his tongue on hers. A shiver raced through her body. He'd delivered her home as promised and she replayed their parting conversation.

"And if I don't show?" she'd asked.

"You swore an oath, so you will." Cole's expression grew grave. "But if you don't learn the necessary information and skills the result will be the same. Most likely death, but not by my hand."

Geez. The man knew how to communicate expectations and consequences effectively.

One of her birds hopped down to a lower branch to get a closer look at Kelly. With Bear back in her life, her number of birds had increased, and the dark Other energy vibrated through the group. Her consciousness zeroed in on this bird's perception.

Kelly sat down across from a man in a cheap suit. The material bunched around his arms and fit loose over his chest. He also left the jacket buttoned even though he sat down. Amateur.

Public defence lawyer, maybe?

If only ravens possessed the ability to distinguish one conversation from many through double paned glass. The meeting lasted an hour and despite the stellar hearing of ravens, she only gleaned a few useless words from the entire conversation.

A bust. Ugh.

Kelly stood and shook the man's hand. His watch glinted in the sunlight.

Oooo. Shiny.

Focus!

The pair left the café together, but once outside,

they parted ways without a word. Definitely not lovers, then. Nothing about this meeting suggested a clandestine meeting for an ill-fated romance.

Raven had never split her conspiracy to follow two different targets before, but she wanted to try it now. Something about the man ruffled her feathers, and not in a good way. But he wasn't the target. She needed to focus on the job.

The man's profile grew more distant and blurred at the edge of her profile.

Damn it.

Now was not the time for conspiracy experimentation. She was still traumatized from the last time she played around with her power and ended up with a giant raven's leg, complete with a scaly foot and talons, instead of a conspiracy. She also transformed into a giant raven to defeat Lloth and still had nightmares about it.

She let the man go.

Her birds launched into the air and tracked the teacher instead. Preventing the birds from investigating every shiny object as they followed Kelly through town proved the most tedious and attention-sapping aspect of this stakeout. Kelly picked up groceries and returned home. Yawn. What a waste of a day. Maybe she should've followed the man.

After sitting and waiting for Kelly to do something else for an hour, Raven gave up and flew to where she had parked her car. She avoided traveling directly to and from her home.

A man leaned against Jean Claude Grand Am with folded arms and a sneer.

Great.

She swooped her conspiracy behind the neighbouring bush where she'd stashed her clothes. Her Other energy pulled together, merging the birds and consciousness into one being. In a few minutes, she transformed, threw her clothes on and stumbled from the bush to face the Lord of War.

"To what do I owe this *pleasure?*" She fastened her belt and tugged down her shirt.

"You have a twig in your hair." When Bane pushed off the car, metal groaned. "Nice curls."

She scowled and yanked at a small branch sticking from her curls. It snagged. She pulled harder and the stick came free, taking some of her hair with it. *Ouch.*

"We need to talk," Bane said.

"Cole asked you to give me a week."

Bane glared, his dark eyebrows bunched in and his expression grew thunderous. "Cole is not my boss."

"Who is?" Did he have a complaint box?

"The Closer situation is urgent." Luke brushed imaginary dirt off his cuff while he stood in front of the driver's side door.

Maybe she could squeeze by and slip into the car unnoticed and without him making a grab for her? "If Cole thinks it can wait until I'm trained in the ancient ways of dark fae douchery, then it can wait."

Bane folded his arms over his massive chest. "You will never master the intricacies of dark fae dou—the

Underworld—and Cole is too concerned with your well-being."

"That's not a bad thing."

Bane ignored her and continued. "He's too focused on you to realize the severity of the situation."

Cole's parting jab at Bane replayed in her head. Why couldn't the Lord of War deal with the situation? He was supposed to be the badass of the badasses. Or did Odin's peace pact prevent him from acting? The Allfather ordered no unnecessary violence or unprovoked bloodshed on the mortal side of the now-collapsed barrier.

"I think Camhanaich understands the situation perfectly." Rourke's voice spoke from the shadows seconds before the weapon warper stepped into the light.

Raven released a long breath.

"Rourke." Bane spat the name out as if it tasted foul. "Servitude doesn't suit you."

Rourke flashed his jagged teeth and twirled a dagger in his hand as if it was no big deal. His skin pulsed bluish gray and the metal of his weapon flashed.

Her birds perked up.

"I disagree," he said. "I find serving a master who inspires respect deeply satisfying."

Raven's eyebrows shot up. Oh, my. There history here. She should probably run while her guard distracted the big bad fae lord, but like a juicy scene in a soap opera, she couldn't look away.

Bane sneered and stepped toward the other fae. "Do

you honestly think you stand a chance against me?"

Rourke's grin widened. His skin pulsed again as he pushed more power into the now-glowing weapon. "Let's find out."

"You will lose."

Did either of them remember she stood right here? From the way they squared off, she may as well pull up a chair, grab some popcorn and get comfortable.

"Who are you trying to convince?" Rourke twirled a dagger on the tip of his finger. The sunlight reflected off the surface. Either he had calluses of steel or he needed to sharpen his weapon. Or...magic.

Bane snarled.

"I might lose, but it won't be quick, and you won't walk away unscathed. How much damage are you willing to take to pester her?" He nodded at Raven. Oh, look. He hadn't forgotten she existed. Lucky her. "Will you risk scarring that pretty face?"

Bane threw his hands up in the universal gesture for exasperation. "I wasn't harming her."

"Yet."

"Nor did I intend to."

"Yet."

"I wanted to talk," Bane growled.

Rourke snapped his dagger from spinning in the air and sheathed it. "Which you are more than welcome to do once the week ends."

If Bane's glare contained real daggers, Rourke would've been skewered on the spot with no chance to retaliate. Nope. Instead of voicing his displeasure with both of them—the emotion clearly written on his face—Bane threw a portal disc on the ground and disappeared into the red haze the moment it snapped in place.

After Bane removed his negative energy from their presence, Raven turned to Rourke. "How long have you been tailing me?"

He shrugged.

He couldn't possibly follow her while she was in bird form unless he had more skills than she was aware of. Her hair also curled in his presence, so she would've detected him earlier if he'd lurked nearby. He must've staked out the car. Jean Claude stood out, so spotting and following her vehicle wouldn't have challenged him.

"Are you going to follow me in some non-descript car?" she asked. "You may as well hop in with me."

"Not that I don't appreciate the offer." Rourke cast a wary glance at Jean Claude and shuddered. "But it's not you I'm hiding from."

"Could've fooled me." She unlocked the car door and yanked it open.

"The element of surprise is often a much needed advantage in combat." Rourke spoke as if she was an infant. Thanks, bud. Like that didn't rub the wrong way.

"Why didn't you chuck a knife at Bane from the shadows, then?" Raven didn't know much about weapon warpers, but they had the ability to ensure their aim was true. They only had to see their target.

"So blood thirsty."

"Well, you gave away your 'much needed element of surprise' and I want to know why." Despite the frigid touch of impending winter in the air, heat wafted from Jean Claude's interior, filled with the stale scent of potato chips.

"If I waited until he hurt you, anything I did would be too late. He could easily whisk you away in a portal before I could react."

"And if you didn't wait?"

"I would start a war on Cole's behalf and my life would be forfeit for the error."

"Oh."

"That's assuming I was successful, though. Even with the element of surprise, I doubt my dagger would touch the Lord of War. He's gifted with a touch of precognition and is a formidable opponent. He wasn't wrong. I wouldn't win in a battle between us. I'd inflict damage before my demise. Few can beat him one on one."

"Who could?"

"Odin, naturally. Probably Huginn Muninn, Erebus and Chaos, and maybe Cole. Camhanaich is one of the few who could stand against Bane. That's why Bane hates him so much."

"I think this is the most you've ever said to me."

"Words can mislead. Actions don't."

"Speaking of actions...About earlier? With those two men in the alley? Thank you. I should've thanked you earlier, but..."

"I'm scary?"

"Pretty much."

Rourke flashed his pointy teeth again, reminding her of the wolf from *Little Red Riding Hood*. He pushed Jean Claude's door shut before she could climb in.

"Forget your car," he said. "You can come with me."

"Why?"

"You're late for your lesson."

Chapter Sixteen

"Cynicism is an unpleasant way of saying the truth."
~ *Lillian Hellman*

The spiraling chaotic energy of the Underworld slipped from her grasp. Sweat dripped from her skin and the cotton shirt stuck to her body. Her jeans clung to her thighs and not in an attractive way. If flying banshees attacked right now, she'd die because she'd be writhing on the ground like a bacon wrapped sausage, stuck in her own clothes.

"I suck at this," she stated.

"Phenomenally," Cole said.

They sat alone on plush cushions under a gazebo

with long sheer drapes. A gentle Shadow Realm breeze wove through the night and teased the gossamer material. The drapes fluttered and flapped in the night-bloom scented air, dancing along with the willowy branches of the nearby trees on Cole's estate.

"Can I learn something else?" she asked. "Maybe how to throw some lightning bolts or give a real-life death stare?" The shifting shadows of corvid energy pulsed inside her, testing the cage.

"Your best chance at survival right now is fleeing. You need to learn how to manipulate your own power to create a portal." His deep voice slid over her shoulders and wound around her body.

Raven pulled the hem of her shirt out and peeled it from her damp skin. "I don't understand how a portal works or what it has to do with the Shadow Realm or my new job." She used air quotes for the last word. If it didn't pay money, it shouldn't be called a job. "And don't get me started on that scythe."

"It's just a weapon."

"Then why does it calm the shadowy energy inside me when I hold it? Why does it stop the restlessness at night?"

"You sleep with your scythe?"

"Don't you?"

A sly grin spread across his face. Uh-oh. Nope. Not going there. No sexual innuendoes or flirting with silken drapes billowing in the wind under an exotic night with dark magic weaving around them. Nope.

"Why don't we take a break?" she said. "You can

give me a theory lesson."

"I'd like to give you something, but it's not theoretical."

"Focus! Oh, Great and Powerful Lord of the Darkness." Raven spoke more to her racing heart and overactive imagination than to Cole.

He scowled.

"What makes the Shadow Realm different than the others? How do I fit in with all of this?" She flung her arms out.

"First, you must understand that Mortal Realm textbooks don't have all the information and are often incorrect. They list the Shadow Realm as a part of the Underworld, like War and Lust, for example, but that isn't exactly true. The Shadow Realm is unique in that it was forged from both the Realm of Light and the Underworld. It is both and neither at the same time. It connected the two realms, and when the barrier collapsed, the magical pressure caused by the sudden access to the Mortal Realm pushed out the shadows to fill the cracks. Now, the Shadow Realm connects all the realms."

"So, if the Mortal Realm, Realm of Light and the Underworld were islands in the middle of the ocean, the ocean would represent the Shadow Realm?"

Cole chuckled, deep and rumbly. "That's one way to put it."

"And to get from one island to another, you have to get wet?"

Cole nodded. "In order to travel from one place to

another, one must navigate the shadows."

"But that means..."

"Without the Shadow Realm, portals are not possible."

"At all? What did they do before portals?"

Cole pressed his lips together and took a deep breath before answering her question. "Only the truly powerful are capable of ripping seams through reality to travel without a shadow based portal."

Guess that answered her question. In a way. "So, the Shadow Realm makes travel between all realms possible, and more readily available to all fae, not just the super powerful. Didn't that piss off the super powerful?"

"Not really. Ripping reality seams requires a huge expenditure of energy and leaves one vulnerable."

Hmmm...speaking from personal experience? Exactly how powerful was her lord...the Lord of Shadows?

"The super powerful are realistic. This is more convenient for everyone." He leaned back against a giant pillow. "And allows them to extend their own reach more efficiently."

She brushed a stray curl from her face. "And if someone controls the Shadow Realm, they control travel between the realms." Her brain traveled down a yellow brick road with wild abandon and ambivalence toward the awful prize at the end.

"Not someone. You."

That was what she was afraid of. A shiver wracked

her body. She ran her sweaty palms down her pant legs. "Well, we're doomed then. I don't know the first thing about being a gatekeeper and my knowledge of border security is limited to a reality television show from a few years ago."

Cole smiled, patiently, like someone did toward a toddler spouting unintelligible gibberish.

She squashed the urge to lunge forward and push him into the pillows. She'd give his smiling mouth something else to do.

Oh no.

That wouldn't do. She needed to keep her mind clear, focused and not consumed with Cole-based fantasies. Time to change tactics. "Why wouldn't you want this role? You'd gain even more power and influence."

"With great power comes great responsibility," Cole said.

Did he even know who he quoted? "You need to stop watching superhero movies."

"You need to start practicing." Cole leaned in, bringing his delicious scent with him, and smiled wider.

Her heart raced. Did he know the devastating effect he had on her? "I need to know why."

He sighed.

"Seriously. Are you fattening me up for the slaughter?" Was his attraction to her all a ruse—a simple plot to make her compliant enough to do his bidding?

He shook his head. "I have enough power as it is, and it never brought me joy." He hesitated as if he wanted to add something and thought better of it. "Adding this mantle only restricts me. It would limit the mobility and ease in which I move between realms unseen."

His words made sense, kind of, but there had to be more to it. Did he not trust her with the information? Not want her to know for more nefarious reasons? Or did he think she was so stupid she wouldn't understand the intricacies of the Underworld?

"So, I need to break up my essence to merge with the Shadow Realm and reform?"

"Yes. It's easier if you're travelling to a place you've been."

"Like here?"

"Yes."

"When I shift, I lose all my clothes. Will that happen when I form a portal as well?"

His smile grew. "All the more reason to visit me instead of some stuffy location in the Underworld."

She gripped the pillow and chucked it at his head.

He batted the pillow from the air with a band of shadow.

Raven highly doubted she'd find any location in the Underworld boring. Traveling to Lust with Cole, for example? The Underworld represented temptation—present company included.

When mortal physicists discovered an additional force allowing them to move past the confines of the physical world, they destroyed the barrier safeguarding vulnerable mortals from the salacious promises and nefarious plans of the dark fae.

Despite the scientists' ingenious method of dismantling the barrier, they lacked the skill or knowledge to reconstruct a new divider to safeguard the powerless mortals. Their notes, lab manuals and journals disappeared in the aftermath of what came next—a true, real-life disturbance in the force.

When the barrier had been intact, the vicious entities from the Other Realms who'd inspired myths, legends and religion bided their time, forced to be content with temporary, short-lived forays into the Mortal Realm before their very nature pulled them home. Once the barrier fell, however, Others invaded, and chaos ensued.

Rumours persisted of hidden documents—this paper, that manual—from the original scientists. Most fanatics spoke about the Murdock Manual, a journal from one of the lead physicists responsible for the barrier collapse, which supposedly contained information to reform the barrier. Regulators whispered tons of "what ifs" but nothing ever came from those rumours and the need for a permanent divider dissipated once Odin stepped in. He demanded peace and compliance, and the warring factions reached an uneasy equilibrium.

Though the events happened generations ago, trust had never fully developed. Not all Others harboured ill-intent, but they all had their own agendas and plans for the easily led and corrupted mortals, affectionately referred to as regs. The difficulty lay in figuring out which group a fae lord fell into.

Cole leaned in and frowned, his dark gaze studying her face as if committing every freckle to memory. The wind tussled his ink-black hair.

"What?" She pulled a fuzzy pillow onto her lap and ran her fingers through the long silky fibres. Who did Cole's home decorating? And why did that thought make her veins turn to ice?

"I don't like seeing you so pensive."

Definitely not admitting concern about who did his personal shopping. "Well, I'm sorry. I don't think I'm going to be taken very seriously if I show up at meetings on mass destruction with the Underworld's finest wearing only my birthday suit."

"You will learn how to deconstruct and reform your clothes as well. But we start with the important bits."

Raven sighed. That's what she was afraid of.

Cole straightened and wove bands of shadow around them. "Theory class is over. Let's practice again."

"Do we have to?"

"You need to be open to learning, Raven. You're planning to go back to school, and you need to assume your role as the Corvid Queen. You can't have a closed mindset."

"What does that even mean? You sound like my high school math teacher." Memories of parent-teacher meetings flooded her mind and sent chills down her limbs. Sure, she tended toward stubborn, but did Mrs. Lesley really have to call home after Raven called an assignment stupid for a third time?

"It means, if you believe you can't do something, you won't be able to do it no matter how much anyone else tries to help. You need to change your mindset first before any learning can take place." Yup. Definitely heard that somewhere before.

"So instead of saying I can't make a portal...?"

"Say you don't know how to make one yet or say you *will* learn to make a portal." The bands wove faster and faster, thicker and thicker around them, whispering against her skin and creating a tunnel-like wall to block out any distractions.

"Yes, sensei."

Cole frowned. "You're lucky you're so cute."

"Cute?"

He frowned harder. "Is that not an acceptable compliment for a Mortal Realm woman?"

"Depends," she said.

"On what?"

"On what you want."

Lightning flashed through his gaze briefly before his expression hardened.

Okay, then.

Chapter Seventeen

"Just think of how stupid the average person is, and then realize that half of them are even stupider."

~ George Carlin.

Raven pivoted in the server area and placed the coffee carafe back on the counter. *Do not hit the customers. No hitting the customers. Don't do it, Raven. It's not their fault they've asked the same stupid question as the last five tables. Deep breath. You need this job.*

"Will you watch my section, Love?" Suzy smacked her gum loudly. "I'm going out for a smoke break."

"Uh?" Raven stopped mentally pep-talking and

scanned the restaurant. Was Suzy crazy? They were in the middle of a rush for once. Well, the tail end of one anyway. Suzy had taken all the orders and now it was a matter of running out the food and ensuring customer satisfaction. What a lovely time to play the smoker card.

Raven didn't have anything personal against smokers. If Suzy used her actual break time to suffocate her lungs that was one thing. But no. She took additional breaks for her vice. As a non-smoker, Raven didn't get the same job perks. Guess she had another pet peeve to add to her growing list.

Raven made lists for everything. At one time, she considered her habit an odd personality trait independent of her family, but after learning her biological father was the combined human form of Huginn and Muninn, Odin's ravens, she wasn't so sure. The birds represented thought and memory, after all. And making lists helped her remember things and aligned her thoughts. But she didn't have the time to delve into the ramifications of her biological parentage.

"Thanks." Suzy waggled her fingers and pulled a pack of cigarettes from her apron on the way to the back exit.

Motherfucker. Maybe Raven should take up smoking to get an extra break or two. She still reeled from her training session with Cole. At the end of the grueling five hour lesson, she was no closer to forming a portal or determining Cole's true feelings toward her. She needed some extra thinking time and rest.

Snuggling the scythe at night only carried her so far.

She wiped her brow with a greasy forearm, grabbed two menus and made her way to the couple who chose a booth on the far side of the room.

First date. And awkward, if the body language was any indication.

Raven slid the plastic covered menus over the recently cleaned table surface and recited the specials and features. The couple asked for waters and time, and Raven left them to their stilted conversation.

Mike said earlier he had some information, but they hadn't had a chance to speak privately with Suzy around. After checking in with the other tables and running out some orders, she walked behind the counter and peered through the kitchen service window. Mike was busy flipping burgers, with sweat running down his face. His cast had turned beige. Raven opened her mouth to grill him for details but the back door on the other side of the kitchen opened. Raven shut her mouth.

A few minutes later, Suzy shuffled into the server's area, dragging in cool air from outside. Cigarette smoke clung to her clothes and pooled around her. Suzy adjusted her apron around her thick waist. Fine, wispy hair created a halo of frizz around her temples.

Raven didn't particularly like Suzy. Something always grated her nerves, but she couldn't quite name it. The smoke breaks were just an added annoyance.

"Thanks, doll. Any issues?" Suzy asked.

"No. You have a new table. I brought them water

and menus, but they needed more time when I checked on them."

Suzy strained her neck to peer over the other diners. "First date?"

"Definitely."

"Going well?"

"Not really."

"Balls."

Mike slid two plates across the kitchen window and left them under the warming lights. "Your table ten is up, Suzy."

"Thanks, sweetie."

Mike scowled. He hated terms of endearment and thought Suzy called him names to piss him off.

Honestly, the older woman probably couldn't help herself. She called everyone something.

"Okay, well, Mike and I are going for a break. Cover me?" Raven said.

Suzy spun around, mouth open, jaw slack. "You already had your fifteen."

"Yeah, I just need a quick, non-smoking break. We'll be back in a second. Holler if I get a new table in my section." Raven walked around to the kitchen and grabbed Mike's arm. She glanced at Suzy from the other side of the service window. She stood in the exact position, mouth still gaping open.

"Thanks!" Raven kept the cheer in her voice and tugged on Mike's arm.

He chuckled and followed her to the back. She pushed open the heavy security door and more cool air rushed in. She welcomed the bite in the air.

Mike's sigh behind her bordered on a moan.

They sat on the top step. If there were an Olympic event for synchronized sitting while sighing, they would've won.

"Not that I don't love the idea of a non-smoking break, are you sure it's wise to piss off Suzy?"

"It's Suzy," she said.

"You know she's banging Dan, right?"

"Ew!" Her entire body cringed at the sudden visual pounding away in her brain. "Since when?"

Mike leaned forward to rest his forearms on his knees. The security light from above beamed off his kitchen whites in an otherwise dark alley and made her brother look like some sort of down-and-out angel. "Not sure, but if you're wondering why she didn't get fired for helping herself to the crab cakes, now you know."

"Now I know..." Raven shuddered.

"Because she gave her crab cake to—"

Raven held up her hand to get him to stop. "Please don't."

A wide smile spread across his face.

Banshee's bastard. If she didn't distract him fast, he'd never stop. "You said you had something to tell me?"

Mike bobbed his head and pulled out his phone from the back pocket. "I looked up black spinel for you since I know you've been too busy to run a web search."

141

Was that sarcasm? Hard to tell with Mike sometimes. He could've texted the information, so he wanted to give her theatrics. Lovely.

Mike cleared his throat and read from the notes on his phone. The lighted screen illuminated his face in the dark alley. "Black spinel is a single refractive stone valued for its natural state. Though rare and gaining popularity, this mineral is relatively affordable."

"What the fuck does relatively affordable mean?"

Mike shrugged. "According to the online auction sites, anywhere from ten dollars to ten thousand."

They fell into silence, both staring at the brick wall of the building across the alley.

"Maybe I should get it appraised?"

"I wouldn't trust the trolls with a mysterious gem gifted to you by some random customer."

Good point.

"Should we go in?" Raven broke the silence. The autumn air had cooled her down.

"Probably. I wouldn't put it past Suzy to steal tips in addition to crab cakes."

"Can you please stop saying crab cakes? I'm getting all sorts of traumatizing visuals."

Mike bounced to his feet and yanked open the door. "Fine. There's no need to get *crabby* about it."

Raven clambered to her feet and followed. Warm air filled with the strong smell of greasy meat and French fries hit her face. "You're awful."

"You love me."

Raven opened her mouth, and then shut it again.

He wasn't wrong. "Guess it's true what they say."

"What's that?"

"You can pick your friends, but you can't pick your family."

Mike barked laughter, his mischievous fox flashing in his gaze. "Please, like you wouldn't choose to join Team Crawford."

Raven forced her tired limbs and heavy feet to carry her back to the restaurant.

"Odin's nutsack. You're right. There must be something wrong with me." She walked through the kitchen double doors and let them swing closed behind her, but not before Mike's final jab.

"You're just figuring that out now?"

If they weren't at work, she'd find the nearest item not nailed down and chuck it at him.

Chapter Eighteen

"Humanity I love you because when you're hard up you pawn your intelligence to buy a drink."

~ *E. E. Cummings*

Raven and Mike staggered into the cool night air from the back entrance of Dan's Diner and let the heavy metal security door slam closed behind them. Mike turned to yank on the handle, tugging on it a few times. The door rattled, but the lock was engaged.

Good.

Night routine finished, they stepped from the lit platform and into the inky darkness.

"Man, I'm glad today's over." Mike slung his backpack onto his shoulder.

Before Raven moved back home, he'd ride his bike to work, but now he chose to leave it home so they could walk together.

"I'm glad we had the earlier shift. I can actually get some sleep." She stretched side to side with her arms in the air.

Mike nodded. His phone pinged and he pulled it from his pocket as they walked down the alley toward the brightly lit street with fast moving traffic. Their shoes splashed in shallow puddles left by the recent rain.

Mike grimaced, the planes of his face barely discernable in the deep shadows.

"What is it?" she asked. Mike couldn't hide the truth from his expression if she paid him to. He sucked at poker. His honesty was one of the things she loved most about her baby brother.

"Looks like your night isn't over." He turned his phone, the screen facing her.

The grainy camera feed showed Kelly leaving her house, face painted on and dressed for what looked like escort service.

Raven snorted. "Hurt her back at work, my ass."

Mike grinned. "Pics or it didn't happen."

"Ugh." This footage wasn't enough to condemn Kelly, and dressing up and putting the girls on display didn't necessarily mean she had joined an escort service. Hell, Raven had worn an outfit just as risqué to hit the clubs with Megan back in their early twenties. But...Raven hadn't put in a fraudulent work injury claim.

"You'll need to shift here if you want to catch her." Mike glanced around and eyed the grimy alley. His lip curled down with the same disgust Raven felt. "I'll take your things home."

She sighed. This case might not end tonight. Her ravens couldn't exactly snap a photo and the Canadian court system deemed any testimony from a shifter witnessed in their "altered" form inadmissible. Politicians still believed shifters lacked the ability to discern facts from fiction when they turned furry, despite all evidence supporting the truth. Haters.

Raven held her hand out and twirled her finger in the air. At least she no longer had to worry about leaving a loaded gun in her purse. After the alley attack, she'd given the sig back to Mom. She couldn't afford to hesitate if or when someone else decided to come for her.

Mike turned and faced the busy end of the alley. He placed his hands on his hips as if to provide more cover than his lean frame. It helped.

She slipped off her clothes, tucked her underwear into her pants before folding them, and called the energy of the Underworld. It soaked into her bones and ripped her apart. Pain rippled through her consciousness as she separated into a conspiracy of ravens.

She swarmed past Mike, batting him with her wings

and swooping by his head. One raven perched on his shoulder and rubbed her head on his cheek. Mike smiled and scratched the back of her neck.

Ah. That's the spot.

"Go," Mike said. "You don't want to miss her."

She head butted her brother's cheek and launched from his shoulder to rejoin the conspiracy. Like a hive mind, she directed the group of birds toward Kelly's house. They arrived in time to watch Kelly's sleek black car pull away from the curve. Perfect. Time to follow.

The drive took forever—Kelly left her neighbourhood and, venturing to the less than savoury section of downtown Vancouver, hit every light on Hastings Street.

Why downtown?

Rife with pawn shops, strip clubs, seedy bars and dealers, elementary school teachers didn't frequent this area late at night. Alone. Sure, she might plan to meet up with some friends for drinks at a high-end bar, but Raven didn't get that vibe.

So, what was it? Drugs? Prostitution? Gambling?

Kelly parked behind a three-story concrete box of a building. Half the conspiracy watched the vehicle while the other group flew to the other side. She'd never split her conspiracy to follow two different targets before, but she could direct her birds to surround different parts of a building as long as they weren't too far apart.

Orange neon lights flashed around the business

sign.

Though the sign and blacked out windows gave nothing away regarding the events taking place inside, Raven didn't need to investigate further. Raven knew this place. '

The only strip club named after a billiards ball in town, the establishment had a robust and notorious reputation.

Last week, a high-profile Hollywood celebrity got busted for cheating on his wife with a stripper from this "gentlemen's club." And last month, a well-known conservative politician from the states had a heart attack in the backroom during a private lap dance.

A gust of cold air ruffled through her conspiracy's feathers. As one, the birds puffed out their plumage against the chill and pulled their heads down from the wind.

Kelly moonlighted as a stripper while collecting loss of income wages due to workplace injury benefits.

At least that's what it looked like. They still needed proof. Raven couldn't exactly direct the conspiracy into the strip club undetected, and even if she did, her testimony wouldn't stand up in court.

At least they knew Kelly's destination.

Oooo. Shiny. One of her birds dove toward Kelly. An image of a shiny silver pendent on a necklace flashed through her collective consciousness.

The other corvids turned their beady eyes toward the target.

No! The bird swooped up at the last second,

narrowly missing the large purse swung in its direction.

"Fucking bird!" Kelly scowled at the raven before tugging down her skirt and knocking on the back door.

It swung open in half a heartbeat and a large bouncer with biceps bigger than Raven's head peered out at Kelly. Thudding music spilled out into the alley from the open door.

Okay, then. No sneaking through that entrance. Raven had no desire to tussle with that guy.

Kelly swiveled her hips past the bouncer. He checked out her ass before slamming the door closed.

Well, at least this signalled the end of Raven's night. She was done. If she had any hope of surviving another training session with Cole, she needed a good night's sleep. And a cold shower.

Chapter Nineteen

"I always say shopping is cheaper than a psychiatrist."
~ Tammy Faye Bakker

Raven stepped away from the heat of Cole's body and out of his embracing arms to walk into her softly lit basement room. The scythe resting on the plush duvet on her bed glowed in greeting before returning to its innate state. Her head still spun from the portal jump and despite Cole's specific instructions, she still didn't know how to form her own. The shadowy magic pulsed inside her, as if taunting her with her own incompetence.

"It will come." Cole's deep, gravelly voice spoke

somewhere behind her.

Right now, after working in such a close space with the Lord of Shadows and his intoxicating scent, the only type of coming she was thinking of was not what he referred to.

Saturday night and at least part of her wanted to party.

She turned to face Cole, his expression an impenetrable mask.

"And if I don't get it? What then?" She knew the answer. Impending doom. Some dangerous dark fae from the Other Realms would wipe her out and she could only hope her family wouldn't be hurt in the process.

"I will protect you." Cole's deep voice rumbled and filled the room with his promise. "And your family."

Raven flopped in one of the armchairs. Her jeans stretched as she crossed one leg over the other. "You can't guard us my entire life, Cole. Even you have limits."

In black leather and fighting garb, Cole appeared every inch the assassin he was. Dangerous. Lethal. Mine.

Mine?

Cole snarled. "I will protect you."

Okay, then. He missed her point entirely, but she dug his macho overprotective act. She rested her arms on the chair and her head on the backrest. "Why?"

His gaze flashed, like lightning streaking through the swirls of shadow. "You know why."

She shook her head, soft curls brushing her cheek. She could get used to this new hair...when it wasn't frizzy.

"Are you planning to use me when I become the Corvid Queen?" She had to ask, even if it came across whiney and insecure, but she cringed at her words.

Cole tensed. "Do you think so little of me?"

"No. Not really. This is more about me. I don't trust my judgment. I've made mistakes before."

"I'm not a mistake." Cole's shadows rose up and swirled around her. "You asked for space. I'm trying my best to respect your wishes."

"But?" Her heart sped up.

"When you look at me like that, you make the task incredibly difficult," he said.

"And if I no longer wished for space?" She pushed off the chair to stand, a tangible need to move closer to Cole wiping away her exhaustion.

Raven spent too much of their time together dancing away from Cole, but her reasons for distance kept getting weaker and weaker. If she were completely honest with herself, the real reason she hadn't acted on any of the openings he gave her was simple. She was scared.

He sucked in a breath and stood absolutely still.

"You once told me you wanted me. Has that changed?" She forced air into her lungs. She couldn't hold her breath now. If she passed out, she'd miss his answer.

He'd certainly learned the extent of her

incompetence since his declaration. Ineptitude rarely worked as a turn on.

"Why would it change?" he asked. "Why do you think I've gone to such lengths to protect you and your family?" His inhuman gaze flashed with swirls of gray before the entire iris turned black and bled out to cover the whites of his eyes. "It's all for you."

If he had other things to tell her, she didn't hear them. Already close, she rose up on her toes and planted her mouth on his.

Cole groaned and held her in his strong arms. Her thin basic cotton T-shirt provided a negligible barrier to his hard intricately patterned leather armour. The ridges of the design and seams pressed into her breasts and stomach. Everything was hard where she was soft.

The seductive forest scent surrounded her. He tasted of mint and power. The shadows caressed her body and stroked her inner thighs.

Mmmm yes. She moaned into his mouth and he deepened the kiss, pulling her closer.

"Finally! You're ho—Ahh!" Mike hollered from the doorway.

Raven broke away from Cole so fast she stumbled back. Flailing her arms like a hatchling on its first flight, she staggered a few steps before regaining her balance. She spun and glared at her brother.

He stood in the doorway, shielding his eyes with his hands. The smell of the spaghetti Mom had cooked earlier rushed in from upstairs.

Her stomach growled.

"Dude, knock!" she said.

"Dude, put a sock on the door handle," Mike shouted back. "Like normal people."

Raven snorted. She was a lot of things, but normal wasn't one of them.

"You can stop covering your eyes. You've only been temporarily blinded, and the danger has passed," Cole said, dryly.

Mike dropped his hands and scowled at Cole. "Thank you, oh Gracious Lord of Shadows."

Cole's gaze narrowed and his shadows pooled around him. Mike didn't seem intimidated with who he scolded, and he should be. If he had any common sense, he wouldn't make a peep. Cole's constant presence didn't make him any less dangerous or volatile, it only acclimatized her family to his company and normalized his behaviour. They still needed to learn more about him. She needed to learn.

Raven stepped between the two men. "What's up, Mike?"

In his everyday attire, jeans and a T-shirt, Mike stood at the door with one foot in and one foot out, wearing a scowl and a whole lot of judgment on his face. "Our other job stepped out again tonight."

"Did you follow her?"

Mike's mouth twisted down. "Yeah and lost her. I cut ahead to the strip club, but she never turned up."

"How long did you hang out in the titty bar and wait?" Raven asked, already knowing the answer.

Cole chuckled softly behind her.

Mike's frown disappeared. "I'm very thorough with my job, Raven."

"I bet."

"Anyway. She never turned up. We could've used you. If I'd known you were off necking with the Lord of Evil over here, I would've cursed your name more."

"Liar," Raven said. Mike wasn't nearly as put out about this entire situation as he pretended.

Mike cast Cole another dark look and slipped out of the room. The door clicked shut behind him.

"He knows he's your baby brother, right?" Cole stepped forward to stand beside her.

Raven turned to find a thoughtful expression on Cole's face, not one plotting her brother's demise. Maybe she was wrong to fear he'd retaliate for minor slights.

Or maybe she should fear him more. If Mike hadn't interrupted them... She shook her head. "Would you rather Bear give you the gears?"

Shadows swarmed around Cole and his face darkened. Guess that was a no.

"Don't worry, I'll get my revenge when Mike finally brings home a girl." Raven smiled.

"You're a patient woman."

Hah! He had Mike's number. "That's twice in a short timeframe I've been called something I'm most definitely am not."

Cole's dark brows rose. "What was the first?"

"Normal."

Cole's full lips split to reveal his perfect white teeth.

Being abnormal had never been a good thing growing up, but right now, the way Cole looked at her like she was the last strip of bacon on his plate sent all sorts of warm tingling sensations through her body.

"What am I, then?" she asked.

Cole hesitated. He started to say something and stopped. He took a deep breath and pulled a dark velvety jewelry case from an inside pocket.

Her heart skipped a beat.

Cool it, Crawford. He's not proposing.

And why would she think a proposal was a possibility? They hardly knew each other. Even though her heart had latched onto Cole like a kid with a lollipop, an edge of mistrust still lingered on the periphery of her feelings for the dark fae lord.

"You are so much more than you give yourself credit for," he said. "I hope you don't mind, but I had your gem mounted so you could wear it." He flipped open the lid to the case. Nestled in the middle of black velvet sat her light absorbing black spinel. A beautiful silver chain and setting contrasted sharply with the austere stone.

Oooo. Shiny.

"You stole my rock," she whispered. Her fingers itched to reach out and touch the stone. Her raven essence perked up, beady eyes watchful.

"Technically, Rourke stole your rock."

She glanced at him. When and how had he done that? Sneaky bastard. She'd placed it in a jewellery box on her dresser. Then again, she hadn't stared dreamily at it for a number of days, almost as if someone had placed some sort of aversion spell on it. "Rourke snuck into my bedroom armed with spells and stole my stone on his own?"

"At my command," he conceded.

She probably should be upset at the invasion of privacy, but the shiny silver chain and light absorbing gem swung in front of her and stole her breath away. "It's beautiful."

"May I put it on you?"

Right now, she'd agree to anything he wanted to put on her. Not trusting her voice, she gathered her long black hair and pulled it out of the way while she turned around.

Cole stepped close, his scent and heat caressing her skin. He slipped the chain around her neck, the cool links slid along her skin. The black spinel nestled between her breasts. Its weight pressed against her breastbone, heavy, and not at all cold like she expected. No longer cool to the touch, the stone didn't burn like an ember, either, but it rested against her skin with a perfect temperature, almost as if it heated up on its own to be there and be a part of her.

The clasp clicked and Cole leaned in, his breath fanning her hair. "*Saol fada agus breac-shláinte chugat.*"

"What does that mean?"

"It's an Underworld expression for good luck."

Raven turned around to find an odd expression on his face.

"What?" he said.

"You honestly want me to believe Others go around wishing each other good luck."

His eyes narrowed. "We're not heartless."

"Not all of you, anyway."

He dipped his chin. "You have a lot to learn about the hearts of Others, Einin."

What in the blazing Underworld did he mean by that?

The shadows rose around Cole and engulfed him before she could question him further.

Gah!

Chapter Twenty

"I believe in looking reality straight in the eye and denying it."

~ *Garrison Keillor*

Raven kicked a stone from her path on the sidewalk and rounded her shoulders against the cool fall breeze. Under her shirt, the black spinel thumped against her chest with each step. With a shiver, she pulled up the wide collar of her heavy zip-up sweater to block the wind. Damn it. Almost winter jacket time. Layers only got her so far.

Normally, she greeted Sundays with a conflicting mix of emotions. Sure, the day signalled the death of the weekend and heralded the impending doom for the approaching work week, but Raven didn't work a standard nine to five, Monday through Friday job, and Sunday dinner always made up for any negativity trying to peck away at her brain.

Not today.

Today, only doom clouded her thoughts. Today, signalled the end of the week Bane granted her to get her shit together before he set upon her with some otherworldly crap she had no skills or experience to handle.

One week and she hadn't mastered portal forming or using the new shifting shadow energy she gained from killing Lloth. She still cuddled the scythe at night to calm the powers swirling in her body but hadn't gained any badass combat skills to wield the weapon. She felt more attuned to the hunk of metal and polished wood, but that was about it. She'd grown accustomed to the scythe's presence, but she'd more likely hack off her own head than successfully defend her life against skilled assassins from the Other Realms.

Maybe the Lord of War would wait for tomorrow? Practice patience and all that jazz?

It was already noon and she'd walked around all day like a tightly coiled spring waiting for him to jump out from every shadow like one of those clowns in a wind-up box. But nope. He hadn't appeared.

Maybe, he dealt with the situation on his own and no longer required her assistance.

Some of the tension eased from her shoulders.

Maybe she'd make it to Sunday dinner after all. She was only a block away from home. The smell of wet dirt, decaying leaves and the taint of ever-present grime carried on the wind as it rustled the bare trees lining the street.

Pepe bleated in the distance.

"We need to talk." Luke's deep voice came from behind her.

"Eek!" Raven squeaked and jumped back. Her dark energy rose up as her body transformed into one raven after another. Dark power slammed into her and her birds rose in the air. She turned the conspiracy around.

Bane's face scrunched up as his attention flicked between the pile of her discarded clothes and her ravens. "This is..."

Her ravens swirled around, faster and faster, forming a protective barrier against the dark fae lord. The shifting energy pulsed and reached out, grabbing onto a familiar power. Raven's dark magic carried her across the shadowy void between the realms with Bane's last word.

"...unnecessary."

Raven materialized in a sunlit room with a framed painting of a raging ocean staring back at her. Oh no. She knew this painting. She'd seen it before. She knew this place and this room. Tension drained from her limbs.

Sheets rustled behind her. Shadows slid from the corners of the room and pooled around her.

"This is an unexpected surprise." Cole's deep voice

rumbled against her bare skin. "You did it, Einin. I'm proud of you."

She whirled around. Cole sat at the end of the bed, his large form no less intimidating without a shred of clothing. Corded muscles rippled as he slid from the bed and stood. The cool-toned bedroom artfully decorated his backdrop like a fantasy come to life. Her fantasy.

"You're naked," she said.

His lips twisted up while his gaze drifted down. "So are you."

Raven squeaked again and wrapped an arm around her breasts and cupped her crotch with her hand. Seductive forest scented air slid over her bare shoulders.

Cole raised an eyebrow.

Her face warmed. He'd seen it all before and savoured every inch. Her whole body thrummed with memories.

His gaze focused on her breasts. "Well, almost naked."

The now familiar weight of her black spinel necklace pressed against her breastbone, warm and reassuring. At least she hadn't lost that.

Banshee's bastard. She could've lost the necklace. She hadn't thought about that. Normally, she never wore valuables or carried important items in the fear she might have to shift. The sig sat in the gun safe for that very reason. She'd debated keeping the jewel at home, too, but couldn't bear to be apart from it.

Panic streaked through her body. Only she would freak out about possibilities that could've happened but didn't. Ugh.

Another thought pecked at her brain like little tetras in a fish tank. Why did the black spinel stay with her when everything else didn't?

She took a deep breath, clutched the jewel tightly and let the panic fade. She needed to focus on the current situation. "My powers suck. Showing up naked from a portal will hardly inspire fear among my enemies."

Cole stepped closer. His body so near, if she leaned in, her nipples would brush his bare chest. Heat radiated off him. His dark gaze traced lines along her skin. "True. But I'm not your enemy."

"What are you then?" She held still. Could she trust him? She'd already trusted him with her family's lives, her introduction to the dark arts and her body. But could she trust him with her heart?

He leaned down and whispered into her ear, "Definitely inspired."

"And here I thought you were just happy to see me."

Cole straightened and all the playfulness in his expression fled. His shadows streaked across the room and returned with a robe. He plucked it from the gray bands and held it out toward her.

Okay then. Fun time had apparently ended. What made him turn so serious?

"Put this on," he said.

Instead of arguing like she wanted to, she pulled the robe on—its plush softness and new smell cocooned her in warmth. The hem met her mid-thigh and curved to her body. This wasn't Cole's robe. Did he carry spares for random visitors or did this belong to someone else?

"We have company." Cole pulled on dark boxer briefs.

A red portal snapped open and Bane stepped through the hazy light and into Cole's room. He scanned the bedroom and scowled. "Thank you for accepting my portal." Bane straightened and cast a vicious glare in her direction. "Very civilized."

"Of course." Cole's dry voice implied he could be quite the opposite.

Bane's gaze narrowed and he turned to Raven. "We need to talk about the Closers."

"She's not ready," Cole said.

Gee, thanks.

"Of course, she's not ready. She'll never be ready. But she formed a portal which means she can do *something*, given guidance."

"And I assume you're offering your services?" Cole's light tone contrasted the darkening room. He gathered his shadows around him and waited.

Bane straightened and pulsed with red energy. The malevolence of his power made Raven's feet itch to run from the room.

"I'd be the smarter choice," Bane said. "But I doubt she'd thrive under my form of tutelage."

He had that right.

"Who then?" Cole asked.

"You."

"I'm already teaching her."

"Not fast enough."

Cole smirked. "You must be crestfallen with the idea that I control your fate."

"Not at all. I rather relish the idea of you doing my bidding to protect some pathetic half-breed mortal."

They snarled at each other.

"Should I leave you two alone?" Raven asked.

They glanced in unison to where she waited. Though she stood almost a foot shorter than both men and wore a skimpy robe, she tried for an intimidating stance. Seriously? Where did this robe come from? And why did the existence of clothing obviously designed with a woman in mind bother her more than the two dark fae lords beside her squaring off against one another?

Cole's expression softened and his dark gaze raked her body.

Bane's scowl remained unchanged. "Nice robe."

She flashed him the middle finger. "How did you know I'd portal here? You arrived almost right after I did. Have you placed some sort of creepy homing device on me?"

"I'm capable of many things," Bane said.

No. That didn't sound ominous at all. Nope.

Bane's smile was so smug it inspired violent thoughts. If she punched him in the face right now, she'd probably break her hand on his teeth. Assuming she'd even land a strike. The Lord of War probably wouldn't stand there and let her swing. Bastard.

"But not that," Cole cut in.

The lords returned to glaring at each other.

"Where else would a lost puppy go but back to her master?" Bane answered her question without taking his gaze off Cole.

The Shadow Lord growled. His response came out as a garbled snarl of words from the Underworld.

The hairs on Raven's arms stood. Normally, Cole whispered to her in his mysterious Underworld language, calling her pet names and expressing all sorts of naughty fantasies. This though. This was downright hostile. She had no idea what he said but had no doubt it was vicious. He was the Patron Fae of Assassins, and he showed his hand right now.

She shivered.

"You're too invested, Camhanaich." Bane drew back.

Cole's gaze narrowed. The shadows pulled in around him. The temperature of the room dropped.

Bane's face lit up, like an internal inferno burned within. His piercing gaze flashed red and a bloody haze surrounded him.

Nope. This couldn't be good.

"Uh..." Raven stepped between the two men like the idiot she was. "As much as I would love to be collateral damage to whatever pissing match you're having right now, can we hear what Bane wants? I owe him a favour and I'd rather get this over with."

The men turned to her again. Déjà vu.

"Well?" She placed her hands on her hips and gave her best "fuck off with your penny tip" face to Bane. "What do you want?"

Cole sighed and stared at the ceiling. His shoulders dropped, but his hands remained balled into fists. His lips moved silently as if he uttered some sort of prayer.

A slow grin spread across Bane's face. "Thank you, Corvid Queen, for granting me an audience."

Oh dear.

Chapter Twenty-One

"Everything great in the world comes from neurotics."
$\sim$ *Marcel Proust*

Raven stood in front of the dark fae lords and waited for the world to end. When it didn't, she took in a deep breath, the air thick with Cole's intoxicating scent. Bane's, too, but it didn't have the same effect on her.

"What exactly does granting an audience entail?" she asked and winced. Even as she spoke the words, she *knew* she asked the question too late.

Bane's smile widened.

"Let's just say, you'll be late for dinner," Cole said.

Raven groaned. "Mom was making pie for dessert."

Bane's eyebrows rose. "What kind of pie?"

"You're not invited," she said. He crashed their last dinner and she'd been too distraught after the revelations to finish the meal let alone have dessert. No wonder she hated Bane. He made her skip dessert.

Bane shrugged.

"Pumpkin," she said.

Bane scowled. "I never understood the appeal."

"That confirms there's something wrong with you," Cole said.

She flashed Cole a quick smile. He got it.

Bane rolled his eyes so proficiently, Juni would've approved.

"Does this audience count as payment for my favour?"

Bane chuckled and shook his head. "You never specified payment for granting an audience, and you can't decide to charge me for one after the fact, so no, you aren't doing me a favour."

She glanced at Cole and his clenched jaw. His dark look and gathered shadows confirmed Bane's words. Well, damn it. She needed to think before she acted or spoke. She couldn't let Cole do everything for her. She couldn't sit back and let others run her life, nor could she take control and bulldoze her way through situations she had no knowledge of.

Balance.

She needed balance.

And ever since Cole Camhanaich stepped into

Dan's Diner to tell her Bear stole from him, she'd been off-balance.

"As to what I want..." Bane said. "I want you to block the movement of all non-Others entering the Underworld."

"All?"

"Yes."

"Forever?"

"Until we extinguish the threat to our realm."

That last condition left a lot of room for interpretation. "If I do this, I will have paid my debt to you in full."

He nodded.

"I will block the movement of non-Others to the Underworld. You will have forty-eight hours to eliminate the threat. If you don't succeed, my debt to you is still paid and I owe you nothing more."

Bane's expression grew solemn. "I need advanced notice of the blockade, and the forty-eight hours starts once it's successfully in place."

"Agreed."

Bane nodded again. "Agreed. We must bind this agreement." He stepped forward.

Raven flinched. Memories of Cole's particular way of sealing the deal flashed through her mind. No way did she want Bane's mouth cooties.

Bane frowned and glanced at Cole, his pause telling, as if he knew exactly what had transpired between them and like a disappointed father, wasn't pleased with the discovery. "I see you're using every opportunity to flaunt our traditions, Camhanaich."

"If it brings you displeasure then I consider my objectives met." Cole glared daggers at the other fae lord. "Even if I didn't do it for you."

Raven had never appreciated the expression regarding two bulls in a china shop as she did now. If these two decided to actually fight, Cole's room would end up in shambles, and Raven would get trampled.

Bane turned to her, his expression somewhere between exasperated and amused. "There are more ways than one to bind an agreement."

She bit the inside of her cheek to prevent something sassy from spilling out.

Bane slid his hand inside his jacket. The expensive fabric of his suit rustled, and he pulled out a small rope. The ordinary rope looked like it belonged on a dock somewhere except it was too thin and too short. Bane gripped the rope with both hands and held it out horizontally in front of his chest.

How had he concealed a rope the length of his forearm inside his well-cut business suit?

Bane mumbled something in Underworld and tied a knot in the rope. His dark red energy coiled around the threads and vibrated. He paused, made eye contact and held out the rope to her.

She plucked the item from his hand like a soiled sock from Mike's room and hesitated. The rope didn't zap or burn her. Though the malicious red energy Bane enclosed over the knot vibrated, the rope remained cool to the touch. "Even if I knew what you just said, my mouth cannot form those words."

Bane made a long, exasperated sigh.

"Language doesn't matter, Einin," Cole said. "The intent does."

"Oh."

"You need to repeat your promise and tie your own magic around the knot," Cole continued.

"How do I know Bane didn't say something else? Something not a part of the deal."

"Because the binding will not work if our intentions do not match." Bane ground his teeth.

She glanced at Cole. He dipped his chin and remained tense. Hopefully, Cole would say something if Bane attempted to trick her. She didn't want him to swoop in and save her or take over, but a heads up seemed like a reasonable expectation of a lover.

Bane followed her look. "What the fuck did you do this last week? Did you teach her anything or just stare broodingly at her?"

"I don't brood," Cole said.

"It's not his fault," Raven said. "I have a job. The Corvid Queen position pays shit. I have bills. Cole had to train me around my schedule." And she'd taken Saturday night off at the diner. Tossing away her most lucrative shift for a last ditch lesson on portal forming wasn't an easy decision or easy on the wallet.

"If you don't smarten up, you won't have any schedules to worry about," Bane said.

"Thank you, Captain Obvious." Like she needed a remainder of the stakes or any added pressure. Her magic lashed out and snapped around his powerful knot.

Bane's eyes widened.

She gripped the rough ends of the knot and squeezed. "I promise to block the movement of non-Others for the period of forty-eight hours after notifying Bane. The success of Bane's endeavors after this notification have no impact or bearing on this agreement. In exchange, Bane acknowledges my debt to him for a favour owed is paid in full." With a mind of its own, her magic synched to Bane's around the knot and snapped off. In case Bane had any questions to her current mood, she glared at him. "Are we done here?"

Bane stepped back, expression murderous, body tense. "Unless I'm invited for dinner?"

"That's a hard pass."

Bane nodded. "I will be in touch."

And there he went getting in the last word to sound ominous again. Now she had three meals, squarely on her plate—discover what the hell her ex-boyfriend was up to, obtain concrete proof Kelly Clementine submitted a fraudulent work claim and resurrect some sort of portal travelling blockade. What she needed to determine was which of those "meals" contained the poison meant to kill her.

Maybe all of them.

"Now, how the hell do I block portal formations?"

"That's for you to figure out." Bane's teeth flashed. He threw a portal disc on the ground. The object smacked the floorboards and red energy exploded to form a portal. Without another word or look, Bane straightened his suit and adjusted his tie before disappearing in a halo of red. Sucked into the closing vortex, the disc left with the Lord of War.

She turned to Cole. He looked ready to leap into battle in his boxer briefs at the slightest provocation. How much had it cost him to hold back and let her deal with Bane? His mouth twisted as if he swallowed a Sefton beetle.

"You did well," he said.

She ignored the trill in her veins from his compliment. Something nagged her. "Why does Bane use discs?"

"Use what?"

"Those portal disc things."

"They're called lodestones," he said.

"Yeah, whatever. He's supposed to be a big bad powerful dark fae lord but relies on these lodestones to get about. Why can't he travel between the realms like you do?"

"Oh, he can."

"Say what?"

Cole grabbed a nearby shirt resting on the edge of a tufted bench. The fabric whispered against the furniture. He pulled it over his head, the white cotton sliding down his body to cover his abs. "I use my essence to wield the force of magic and travel between the realms, the shadows cut through the barriers. You harness the energy of corvids to do something similar. Think about Bane. Would you really wish him to tap into his particular talent to hitch a ride to run some errands?"

Bane, the dark fae Lord of War. He'd have to harness bloodshed, rage, death, or some other powerful emotion or action associated with war to travel without a lodestone. He'd incite all sorts of violent acts whenever and wherever he travelled. He probably didn't use lodestones out of respect for life or the fear of repercussions, he probably did it to avoid leaving a trail for someone to follow. The lodestones allowed the Lord of War to move more freely and undetected.

Wasn't that a pleasant thought? Her mouth fell open and she gaped at Cole.

"Exactly," he said and finished dressing. "Now, about that pie...Do you think we can make it to dinner?"

Chapter Twenty-Two

"Human beings cling to their delicious tyrannies, and to their exquisite nonsense."

~ Sydney Smith

Raven focused the beady eyes of her conspiracy at the busy café across the street. Her birds' positions on the surrounding trees and buildings gave her excellent vantage points. Kelly sat with the mystery man at a pedestal table by the window. Kelly wore a modest white blouse and black skinny jeans with pumps. Unfortunately, fashion choices weren't enough to charge Kelly with fraud, but if Raven ever hurt her back, she'd be lying around the house in sweats and slippers, not traipsing around in ankle-breakers.

Raven wished she lounged at home in active wear right now. She no longer had any downtime. She either worked at the diner, investigated her cases, or failed miserably at being a dark fae queen in Cole's presence. They had made it to Sunday dinner the other night after Bane's audience and the presence of her family helped leash the burning need to rip off her clothes and slap her body against the Lord of Shadows. Their last two training sessions were fraught with tension, but Raven poured every ounce of effort into focusing on her portal building. Ogling the tutor would not save her life, keep her family safe, or pay the bills.

No more a queen than Dad's goat, she'd switched gears today to follow Kelly on another one of her Wednesday afternoon outings. Kelly met the same guy at the same downtown Vancouver café, but if they were going for inconspicuous, they failed. Who sat at a window seat for a secret meeting? And who was this guy? A sponsor? Dealer? None of Kelly's background checks indicated addiction as a possibility, but that meant little. Some of the most intense addicts were adept at coping and appearing "normal."

Still, this guy didn't look like a dealer, and although sponsors didn't have a formulaic appearance, the gleam in mystery man's gaze gave the same impression as one of those door-to-door missionaries trying to sell their religion. Or an accountant who was super enthusiastic about tax returns.

Her birds leaned in, the cold air rippling their feathers. Was Kelly religious? Was she confessing her sins to her pastor or priest? Maybe next week, if they hadn't closed the case, they could send Mike in with a wire. Kelly pushed away from the table. Her facial expressions and body language typical of a polite farewell. She sauntered out of the café, looked both ways and strolled down the sidewalk away from Raven's position.

The conspiracy vibrated.

Let her go.

Last week, Kelly's events after this outing were uneventful. Not following her now carried a certain risk, but one Raven was willing to pay. Something about this whole case and Kelly's platonic coffee "date" nagged her, like Raven should see a bright flashing neon sign instead of a drab middle-aged man if she looked at this situation at the right angle.

The wind picked up a little, bringing with it a bite as a reminder of the approaching winter and the promise of rain. The air smelled of exhaust, oil and garbage. How did plants still exist in this ravaged world?

The birds puffed out their feathers and pushed their heads down into the protective warmth.

Well, fuck this.

Maybe she should've followed the fraudster. Mystery Man did jack shit.

One by one, she directed the birds to launch off their perches. Sure, she could send them all aloft at the same time, but that would bring more attention than she'd like.

Oooo. Shiny. One of her birds gawked at a shiny medallion hanging from a chain and surrounded by chest hair that would've made the 70s proud.

Who unfastened that many buttons on a shirt these days?

Robert.

A shudder rippled through the collective consciousness of her conspiracy. The urge to dive toward him as a group took every ounce of effort to squash.

Ugh. He still wore that gaudy necklace.

Robert swaggered toward the coffee shop, oblivious to his audience. He stepped in front of a young woman with a stroller and reached forward to swing open the door. The mom beamed at him. Robert stepped in front of her and into the warmth of the café, releasing the door to swing shut behind him. The woman's bright smile faded. At least Robert consistently demonstrated his prowess with the fine art of assholery.

One by one, Raven called her birds back.

The young mom caught the door with her hip and pushed it open. She glared at Robert's back.

Raven's conspiracy perched and watched, all their beady eyes tracking his progress through the café. He moved with purpose and passed the counter.

No.

With a few more steps, he closed the distance.

No.

Today wasn't the second Wednesday of the month. This didn't make sense.

With each step, a sense of dread reverberated through her conspiracy. Robert reached forward and greeted the same mystery man with a handshake.

Raven's two cases collided like two cars at a demolition derby.

The two men sat and discussed what Raven could only assume was some douchebag pumpkin spice latté'd what-the-fuckery topic. The whole while, she sat, fuming while her collective bird brain attempted to connect the dots.

What did this mean? Were Robert and Kelly in some exclusive club for narcissistic losers? Who met weekly? Or were they trying to rehabilitate their sociopathic ways and this really was a sponsor?

Nope. That second one couldn't be true. Robert lacked that kind of self-awareness.

Were they a part of some other type of group? Regulators? Or maybe the more extreme group—the Closers—that Bane kept harping on about?

Raven grew up in the PI business and didn't believe in coincidences.

Sure, she hoped things happened due to random chance, but experience taught her the cold, heartless truth. And the rule of Parsimony. The most obvious answer was usually the correct one.

Unease flittered through her birds like a cold draft along the back of her neck. Too long sitting in one place always made her conspiracy nervous. Predators.

While her conspiracy had grown in numbers, she had no wish to experience the destructive force of a bird of prey snapping the neck of one of her birds. No thank you. It might not kill her or damage her human psyche, but it still hurt.

Robert and the mystery man who looked like a zealot in tweed stood simultaneously and shook hands.

She didn't want or need to see where Robert went despite an intense need to tell him where to go. This time she followed Mystery Man.

He slipped into the back alley and looked over his shoulder. He reached inside his jacket pocket and ducked around the next corner.

Amateur.

As if she'd follow on foot.

Her birds launched in the air and flew over the buildings and ran into a wall of pain.

Chapter Twenty-Three

"It's all right letting yourself go, as long as you can get yourself back."

~ Mick Jagger

Agony streaked through Raven's hive mind like an intense brain freeze on steroids. A vise-like pressure clamped on her collective consciousness and squeezed.

Ow. Ow. Ow.

Her dark energy condensed inward. Her birds absorbed into one and she materialized into her human form on the dirty roof of a downtown east side building

Cold sludge from old rainwater numbed her

exposed skin.

"Oooo." She held her pounding head in her hands. "Not good."

The footsteps of Mystery Man faded into the distance.

Screw this. She reached for her dark energy. Pain exploded along her nerves, again.

Okay, then. No birds.

She stumbled to her feet. Watery grime ran down her naked body and she brushed away the grit clinging to her skin. She needed to get away from whatever interfered with her powers.

She headed to the other side of the roof to the rusted fire escape and glanced down. The alley was empty, but the idea of walking around naked in a less-than-savoury neighbourhood near strip clubs, pawn shops and needle exchange sites didn't strike her as a great idea.

She took a deep breath. She only needed to get far enough away from the blocker to shift. At least that's what she hoped. If the vise-like pressure somehow destroyed or damaged her ability to connect with her Other energy, she'd be devastated.

Odin's nutbar. She'd never fulfill her agreement with Bane if that happened.

What would he do to her if she failed? What would he do to her family? Ice trickled down her spine. Losing her powers was not an option. Not now. Not this way.

She clambered down the fire escape. The ladder wouldn't slide down—too rusted. Crap. She'd have to jump.

She swung over the railing and dangled five feet from the ground. Her hands gripped the cold, wet metal. She looked down.

Why the hell did she look down?

Idiot.

Her hands slipped and she plummeted. Her feet smacked the pavement. Her knees buckled and she rolled. Pain shot up her legs and she clenched her teeth.

"Ow." She peeled herself from the pavement. More muck and stagnant rainwater coated her skin. She smelled only slightly better than the grime clinging to the ground. She straightened, wobbling a little.

"That was a lovely jump." An old craggily voice rumbled from under a soiled blanket.

Raven yipped.

A homeless man huddled under the damp material next to the dumpster. He peered out from beneath long, oily hair. "You shouldn't be out here like that."

"I know." She hesitated. She should ask him about the Mystery Man, but she was naked and in a sleazy area. Yup. Time for clothes.

She turned away from the direction of the blocker and ran. Her boobs bounced painfully, and her ass jiggled. The black spinel smacked against her breastbone.

Rain broke from the sky and thundered down. Fat raindrops splattered against her head and bounced off the pavement. Ice cold, the rain ran down her limbs and washed away the filth.

Running sucked at the best of times but running barefoot and naked was definitely worse. Her feet slapped the wet ground.

She reached for her birds again.

Ow. Ow. Ow.

Pain exploded in her head. She released the corvid essence and staggered to the side. Crap. More running. When her vision cleared and the ringing in her ears faded, she straightened and forced one foot in front of the other, again and again, until she picked up speed.

She turned the corner to the main alley and tried reaching for her dark energy again.

This time she connected. No pain. Her magic rose, fast, furious and dark. It spiraled up like a whirlwind and consumed her. Comforting and reassuring, she embraced her power like slipping into her favourite pair of pajamas. Now she could go home where it was warm, clean and safe.

The power continued to twist and spin. A band of the shifting underworld shadow magic threaded between the corvid energy in the vortex. Instead of splintering into a conspiracy of ravens, she travelled through the shadow dimension and reformed in her basement room.

Warm air brushed against her clammy skin and rain dropped from her naked body onto the short pile carpet. She patted her chest to find the necklace still in place.

"Neat," she said. Her scalp prickled.

"You're getting better at that, Einin."

Raven squeaked and whirled around. Wet hair slapped her face. Shadows slid off Cole's menacing frame to gather in the corners of the room. The soft light hanging from the ceiling highlighted the severe cut of his cheekbones and jaw. His dark gaze flashed.

Odin's shriveled stick, he was devastating to look at.

"Thanks," she wheezed. Uncomfortable pressure wrapped around her chest and squeezed.

"The necklace looks good on you."

She glanced down at the black spinel nestled between her breasts. Droplets of water trailed down her body, following the curve of her chest. "With or without clothes?"

"Both, but I find I prefer this look the most." He stepped forward, all tease fled from his expression, replaced with a need so hot the waves of warmth radiated from his skin. "You smell of the rain."

She swallowed. Her body ached for his touch. She wanted him to take her in his arms and make her nerves sing. She'd barely survived sending him away the first time. If she tasted the sweetness again, would she say no again? Ever? Send him away? Would she want to? Would she need to? His touch was a drug.

"You think too much," he said.

She smiled. "Let me guess. I should just feel?"

He nodded.

She wiped the wet hair from her face. "I'm worried if I let myself feel you again, I'll lose all sense of who I am."

"Then we share the same fear." His deep voice rolled over her like a caress.

Say what? The mighty Lord of Shadows feared something?

He took another step forward. Now, directly under the bulb, the light cast shadows over his face. "What we shared is not a typical experience for me. If I close my eyes, I feel you in my arms. I want you, again and again, even though you sent me away. Giving you time and space has been one of the most difficult things I've ever had to do."

"Even holding my brother in fox form while you watched me scale a tree to break into my parent's place?"

His serious expression cracked a little. "Yes."

"Harder than watching the past Corvid Queen attack me?"

"Definitely."

"Even splicing off sections of the Realm of Light and the Underworld to create the Shadow Realm?"

Cole growled. "Even that."

Her mouth fell open. The pressure squeezed her chest again.

"But the fear of losing myself in the heat of your body is nothing compared to the fear of not being with you," he said.

She shut her mouth and swallowed. His words thawed her heart and cast away the chill in her bones. Her doubts and fears fled with the rising heat from her core. "I often think of you as an addictive drug."

"That's a fitting analogy." He nodded and closed the distance. Warmth still radiated from his skin and the shadows rose from the confines of the room to surround them. "Can't get enough?"

"And the withdrawal is hell."

"Do you still want me to stay away?" he asked. Large and looming, he held back...even now. He still gave her room to breathe, to escape if she wished, but she didn't want to breathe. Not without him.

"No," she said.

With that simple word, he gathered her in his arms. The shadows caressed her skin.

"I'm not sure I can let you go again," he said, his voice holding a hint of warning.

She nodded. She didn't know very much about him or the Underworld. The inner workings, politics, and dynamics were a complete mystery, much like Cole. Why did her Other energy sing whenever he came near and intensified with his touch instead of getting snuffed out like it did with other Others?

Despite so many unanswered questions, Cole was kind underneath his lethal exterior. He was considerate and respectful, and he held himself in check because she asked him to. And even though she ordered him to get lost, he worked behind the scenes to ensure her safety. Rourke was right—words could mislead. Actions didn't. There were no nagging voices in the back of her head trying to warn her like there was when she dated Robert. She had no doubts about Cole as a man. Not anymore.

Cole waited patiently as her brain scrambled, stumbled and clambered to process the truth her heart always knew. She reached up and slid her hand along his porcelain-smooth face. Warm and present and not at all like a granite statue. His predatory gaze remained trained on her, waiting.

"If you let me go," she whispered. "I will crash and burn."

His dark gaze flashed. "Then I won't let you go."

Such a simple solution. She opened her mouth to comment, but Cole's lips closed on hers. The contact sent all remaining thoughts racing from her mind and left only him. Only Cole. Her energy rose up to entwine with his intoxicating power.

"Do you have a sock?" he pulled back to ask.

"A sock? Do you mean a condom?"

"No. I mean a sock. Your brother suggested using one if we didn't want any interruptions."

"Oh." Images of her family flashed through her mine. Ew, no. Gross. Mood killer.

Cole chuckled, pulled her close and wrapped his shadows around them. The dark energy carried them away, through the dimensions between the realms. This time, Raven followed the movements around them and understood the intent of his magic. He seamlessly wove the bands of shadow to move them to the Realm of Shadows.

They reformed in his bedroom.

"Much better than a sock," she said.

He grinned and kissed her again. His hands and

shadows splayed against her, everywhere, running over her body and sliding along her skin.

She throbbed with need. She gripped the hem of his shirt and tugged it upward. He stepped back and let her pull the soft fabric from his body. As soon as the shirt cleared his head and freed his arms, he unclasped his belt and pulled his jeans down.

Oh, my. Commando.

His impressive erection jutted out and Cole stepped from the clothes pooled at his feet. He pulled her close again. Her breasts pressed against his bare chest. His mouth found hers and she lost herself in the feel of his lips and tongue, and the intoxicating forest scent surrounding them.

Chapter Twenty-Four

*"I'm really trying to be fabulous today, but I was so
fucking fabulous last night I'm exhausted."*

~ *Unknown, someecards.com*

Raven attempted not to squirm while Mike
peered at her through the kitchen service
window. Wafts of warm air filled with burger
grease caressed her face.

"You're extremely too happy to be on shift here," he
observed. "What's up? Did you break the insurance
case?"

"No." She knew precisely why a smile kept teasing
her lips and refused to go away. She knew a number of

reasons, and they all began with the letter O.

"Figure out what Robert's up to?"

"Not really." Crap. This direction of questioning wouldn't lead to a desirable destination. Warning! Distract. Divert.

He crossed his arms.

"Something weird happened," she said.

"Oh? Well, spit it out already. We're slammed."

Raven snorted. The diner was empty. "Kelly went to a café to meet the same man as last Wednesday, but this time I didn't follow her when she left."

Mike's eyebrows rose.

"Robert showed up."

His mouth dropped open. "No shit."

"Met with the same guy, too."

Mike frowned. "Can't be a life coach, then. Robert's not the type to realize he's an asshole who needs help."

"I thought the same thing. So, what are they meeting about?" She tapped her finger on the smooth countertop.

The diner door swung open and they both turned toward it.

Bane strode through the entrance with his usual scowl.

Drat. Raven's shoulders dropped. She hadn't seen Cole since this morning, and she was already in need of her next fix. Her body trilled with the memory of his touch and heat spread through her body. Her cheeks grew warm.

Bane's gaze narrowed and he stopped at the

counter. "What's wrong with you?"

"Nothing." Raven patted down her frizzing hair.

"Well?" he asked.

"Well, what?" Raven pulled at the chain around her neck and played with the black spinel as if she had zero fucks to give that the Lord of War had graced them with his presence. On the inside, a war of emotions broke out in a rampage. Pun intended. What did he want? Why was he here? Could she make it to the nearest exit before he seized her? How could she protect Mike?

His jaw clenched. "Any progress?"

"A little, but not enough to make you happy, I'm guessing." Forming a portal twice was a huge accomplishment for her, but her mind failed to wrap around how to block portals completely. Cole kept trying to reassure her, saying once she mastered creating portals, blocking them would be simple.

Somehow Bane's scowl deepened.

"If you're going to keep frowning like that, you're going to get lines. I can recommend a good moisturizer," she said.

He held his hand up for her to stop. Like he'd lose his shit if she kept talking. Yeah, she harboured no secret desires to see that.

She clamped her mouth shut.

Honestly, his expectations of her abilities were too high. She couldn't deal with a blocker to follow some plain-clothes Mystery Man down a downtown Vancouver alley. She snapped her fingers. "Hey.

While you're here and already putting your unimpressed face to good use, maybe you can he— Maybe you can answer a question for me."

Bane grunted.

Guess that was a yes? "Yesterday, I followed a man involved in another case with my conspiracy. I ran into something that caused me a lot of pain."

"You never told me that," Mike said.

She half-turned to address him. "I hadn't got to that point in my story yet."

"Pain?" Bane said, drawing her attention back to him. "I have no interest in hearing you recount your broody romance with the Lord of Shadows?"

She flipped him off. "Whatever it was, it latched onto my Other magic and squeezed my mind in a vise. It was so intense, I had to reform as a human and couldn't access my power until I got far enough away."

Bane's smirk disappeared while she spoke, and his expression grew contemplative. Had he heard of this before? He wasn't mocking her anymore.

"You were...naked...downtown? In an alley?" Mike growled. "Fuck, Raven. Why didn't you say something?"

"Nothing happened. I'm fine." She spoke over her shoulder. "And I was going to say something. I'm saying something now."

Mike grumbled.

"Besides, I wasn't totally naked. I had my necklace on." Her hand drifted down to touch the stone at the end of the necklace.

Mike groaned. "Like that black spinel is going to save you from harm."

Bane's gaze dropped to the pendant in her hands. "Black spinel?"

"Yeah." She held it toward him. "It's a pretty black rock. A customer gave it to me."

Bane's head dropped back and he laughed, loudly. Obnoxiously, even.

She tucked the necklace under her work blouse, placed her hands on her hips and waited for the Lord of War's fit of the giggles to subside. He didn't need to be so condescending. She loved her necklace.

"No simple customer gave you that." He pointed to her chest where the necklace now hid behind her clothing.

The hairs on her arms and the back of her neck stood up. Raven had already recognized the man hadn't been normal, but having Bane state the obvious had dread clambering up her spine like a rabid dog.

"And that's not a simple black spinel."

"Is it complex, like you?" she asked.

Mike's head snapped back and forth to follow the conversation. He needed to be careful. He still had one arm in a cast, he didn't need a neck brace added to his self-care kit.

Bane shook his head. "That's not a black spinel at all."

"What?" She froze.

"That's not a black spinel."

She looked down at her chest. "Yes, it is. The man

said so."

Bane let the silence speak for him. The dramatic pause left only a weird buzzing in her ears along with the oldies playing over the restaurant's speakers.

"And the internet. So, it must be true."

Bane flashed his teeth at her—pretty and perfect, but far from friendly.

Ice flowed through her veins. Cole took an interest in the gem as well and had it set in this necklace. Did he also know what it was? And if so, why hadn't he said anything?

"What is it, then?" she asked.

Bane shook his head and refused to answer.

"It's still a pretty rock," she said, surprised her voice came out even and controlled.

"On that, we agree." Bane leaned against the counter. He cringed and straightened, checking the arm of his expensive suit for damage. "This blocker, you mentioned. It flared up when you were trailing a man? Is he an Other?"

"I didn't get close enough to determine that." Since training with Cole, she'd improved on detecting dark energy at a distance without relying on her hair curling faedar.

"Could he be from the light?" Bane asked, lip curling up in apparent disgust.

Members from the Realm of Light, known as Rollers, rarely sullied their soles by mingling in the Mortal Realm, so she hadn't been exposed to their energy. At least, not that she was aware of. She didn't know if she'd detect Roller energy like she did with beings from the Underworld.

"Doubt it," she said.

"Me, too." Bane's eyebrows pinched in. "Is he a Regulator or a Closer?"

Raven frowned. "I'm not sure what or who he is. He's met with two subjects of two separate investigations."

"There are rumours the Closers developed technology to deter Others. This might be it. Be careful, Raven. It would be unfortunate to lose you before you make yourself useful."

She pursed her lips. "Gee, thanks."

He nodded and strode out of the diner. The door clicked shut behind him and left Raven and Mike in the empty diner.

"And I thought Cole was an asshole," Mike grumbled.

The mention of her midnight lover had her spinning and glaring at her brother. He held up his hands in mock defence. His cast appeared almost brown now. Surely, the doctor could take it off soon.

"Bane is an asshole, but why do you think Cole's one?"

Mike opened his mouth, but she cut him off.

"Because he checked out my ass and saved us from Bane's trap?" she asked.

Mike waved his hand through the air in front of him as if physically swatting away the words. "No. Because he abducted you and planned to torture you for information regarding the previous Corvid Queen that almost led to your death and Bear getting used as some sort of perverted power source."

"Oh, yeah. That." Cole had justifiable reasons for all of those things and did them before he knew her, but when listed together, it sounded bad.

"Yeah. That. And let's not forget he manipulated you into becoming the current Corvid Queen, which puts your life in even more danger."

Manipulated was a strong word.

"And now you're moon-eyed and all wistful, again, which can only mean you've let him back in your pants."

"Ew, Mike. Gross. Don't talk about my pants like that."

Mike grumbled and took a deep breath. "Just promise you'll be careful."

"Like...use condoms?" She raised an eyebrow. She knew damn well what he meant, but if she had to be uncomfortable with this conversation then so did he. "Or use a safe word, or...?"

Mike squeezed his eyes shut and shuddered. "You fucking know what I mean. Don't leap in with two feet. Keep one on the ground."

She clenched her teeth. Now would not be the time to confess to her brother she'd already fallen, and hard. Both feet in and all. He wouldn't understand. Hell, she didn't understand, either.

Mike's expression softened. He shifted his weight and leaned back from the kitchen window. "He makes you happy, though, doesn't he?"

She swallowed and shrugged. "Maybe."

Mike shook his head. "You have the worst taste."

"Is this where I should say something incredibly harsh like at least I have a love life?"

"That would be a douche move." Mike glared. "And no love life is better than a bad one."

"Okay, then. Let's talk about our plan for Friday night and Kelly's next shift, instead."

Mike's face brightened. Yeah. He'd like this plan.

Chapter Twenty-Five

"Everyone knows that if you've got a brother, you're going to fight."

~ *Liam Gallagher*

Raven dove into her car and slammed the door shut on the rain. She reached for her folded clothes on the passenger seat as rain pattered against the windshield. The jeans stuck to her damp legs. Raven cursed and hoisted the stretchy material over her ass and zipped the fly. The shirt tangled and caught on the rear-view mirror. Despite the frigid air outside, sweat broke out over her entire body.

Banshee's tit, getting dressed in a car sucked. Raven

contorted like a pretzel, unhooked her shirt from the mirror and pulled the cotton-polyester blend down to cover her body. Safe in the confines of Jean Claude, she dug her phone out from the secret console under the passenger seat and dialed Mike.

He picked up on the third ring. "Yeah?" Loud bass blasted from his end of the line.

"She's headed in. Are you in position?"

"Oh yeah."

Raven scowled at her phone. "How are you holding up?"

"It's been rough, Rayray."

Hah! Sure. He'd spent the last half an hour sitting in a strip club, banking on Kelly showing up for work. He'd probably have to wait even longer before she made it to the stage. Assuming she was a stripper and not there for something else.

"There is a small hitch in our plan," he said.

"What?" Raven straightened in her seat and stretched her neck. The rain outside stopped as suddenly as it started.

"Sign says no photos or video."

Raven cursed again, but only half-heartedly. Prohibitory signs weren't a surprise. Most strip clubs had the same or similar rule. Sure, taking photos for evidence wasn't against any Canadian criminal laws, per se, but if Crawford Investigations obtained surveillance photos or videos procured from inside the strip club and the prosecution used said evidence to charge Kelly in a court of law, as a private establishment, the strip club could sue Crawford Investigations for violating their rules.

No thank you.

Crawfords were rule followers. Mostly.

"Plan?" she asked.

"Well, I'm not in animal form. If I observe her often enough and we get enough footage of her entering and exiting the club, my testimony should be enough."

"Yeah, but geez. That sucks for you. You're going to have to spend hours watching beautiful women peel their clothes off and dance in front of you. There must be another way..."

Mike laughed and hung up on her.

She threw her phone on the passenger seat and slid the key into the ignition. Jean Claude roared to life. Maybe Cole could whisk her away to the Shadow Realm and make her forget tomorrow existed. Not that she had anything against tomorrow, she just craved the timelessness that overcame her when Cole's single focus in life seemed to make her body hum his name.

Warmth spread across her skin.

Mike's warning replayed in her head. Was she moving too fast? Probably. Was she making the right decision?

She drummed her fingers along the cold steering wheel. The problem with that question was the answer often didn't become obvious until well into the future. Hindsight was always 20/20.

A little reservation wouldn't hurt, and she had another relationship in dire need of mending.

She plucked her phone from the worn seat beside her and dialed a different number.

"Hello?" Her twin's deep voice vibrated against her ear.

"What are you up to tonight?"

Raven shut the car door and winced at the door hinge shrieking in outrage. Jean Claude would never be a stealthy vehicle. Ever.

The cold fall wind breezed by and she stepped onto the sidewalk in front of Bear's building. The trolls who controlled the one remaining bridge to the North Shore allowed favour and fare free travel only one night a week. Tonight, specifically. The troll toll was astronomical on any other given day. Those who lived on the north side, like her brother, found other ways to travel across Burrard inlet during regular days or avoided travelling to the other side altogether.

The sharp tang of the neighbouring forest burned her nose. Her senses prickled as a subtle note of an Other flittered around her. The dark energy pulled at her own and made her scalp tingle.

She straightened. "I don't know where you're lurking, Rourke, but you may as well come out."

He cursed and stepped from the shadows of the nearby alley. The same alley where Cole had thrown her against a sticky wall.

Aww. Memories.

"I wish Cole hadn't taught you how to recognize dark energy signatures. Cramps my style."

She didn't have the heart to tell him she learned how to identify fae energy with her hair curling trick long before Cole. Surely, some dark force joke was in there somewhere, but it would be wasted on Cole's henchman. Most Mortal Realm references were. "Worried about job security?"

"Worried about you giving away my location and ruining the element of surprise."

"It will be easier for you to guard me from inside the building." She swept her arm out in a wide arch at the apartment entrance.

Rourke scowled but walked with her to the front door. "What are your plans?"

"Hanging out with Bear."

"Doing what?"

She hit the buzzer.

"What?" Bear's voice rumbled over the scratchy speaker.

She leaned forward to speak into the small microphone under the speaker and pressed the button. "Prepared to lose?"

Bear didn't reply. He hit the buzzer instead and Raven wrenched open the door.

"You're hanging out with your brother on a Friday night?" Rourke's scowl deepened. "That's sad."

"The troll bridge is free on Fridays."

Rourke grumbled but followed her through the lobby. She veered away from the questionable elevator and headed for the stairs. Her bodyguard's loud, suffering sighs trailed behind her.

Bear opened the door on the first knock with a smile. "Rayray."

His arms circled her for a giant hug.

Mmmph. "Brother Bear."

Her twin froze against her.

Ah, he must've spotted Rourke over her shoulder. Guess it was kind of hard to miss an assassin with jagged teeth.

"I picked up a stray on the street."

Bear remained frozen.

"No, seriously. Cole sent him to guard me, so I invited my babysitter to join us. Don't scowl at him."

Bear released her and stepped back. An expressionless mask slid across his face, but he didn't ask why she had a bodyguard. He didn't need to. He'd realized before she did how much her new role plunked her in danger.

She flung up her hands. "It was that or have him lurk in the shadows spying on us."

Bear stared at Rourke.

The assassin waited, stance easy, expression blank.

"He has to play, too," Bear said.

"Of course."

"Excuse me?" Rourke leaned in, all manners. "Play what?"

Raven pulled her bodyguard into the apartment. He let her, otherwise, he wouldn't have budged. Rourke didn't' seem like the type to go somewhere he didn't want to go.

Bear snorted and closed the door behind them.

Kissa, Bear's demonic cat from hell, spotted Raven at the entrance and hissed.

"What is that?" Rourke said.

"Housecat," she answered. "She hates me."

Kissa continued to hiss, arching her back and hopping toward her, but kind of sideways at the same time.

"Shoo." Raven flicked her hands out.

Ears back, tail down, Kissa streaked into the nearby bedroom.

Rourke watched the entire exchange, his brows furrowed and his mouth twisted down. He shook his head, collected himself and turned to Raven. "So, what are we playing?"

"It's movie night," she answered. "I won last time, so it's my choice. You have to watch whatever movie I choose, and you can't groan, mock or insult the movie or else I win and get to pick again."

Rourke's eyes narrowed. "That's a horrible game. Is everything a competition between you two?"

"Yes," they answered in unison.

"Hey, Bear. Before I forget, can you look into someone's personal finances for me?"

"Personal finances not accessible through legal public inquiry?" he asked.

She nodded.

Bear's eyebrows rose to his hairline. "My, my, Rayray. How the mighty have fallen."

His tone was complete bullshit. Though she followed the rules when working for Dad, Bear knew she bent them sometimes if the case warranted it.

"Who's the person?" Bear asked.

"Robert."

He didn't hesitate to respond. "Consider it done."

Raven nodded and sat on Bear's couch next to Rourke, while her brother took the armchair. He'd already popped the popcorn and brought out the chips. His living room smelled like a cleaner version of a movie theatre. With a side of cat.

Rourke lasted five minutes before he started tearing apart the rom-com Raven strategically selected. Bear made it another three. Accepting their loss, the two decided they couldn't lose any worse than they already had and spent the remaining one-hundred and fourteen minutes proving how truly obnoxious they could be.

A vibrating phone interrupted Raven's laughter at Rourke and Bear's scrunched up faces. Mike's face popped up on her screen.

"Hey," she answered.

Bear leaned forward and snatched the remote from the coffee table.

"It was rough, but someone had to do it," Mike said.

Raven snorted. "Did you witness enough?"

"Oh yeah. There's nothing wrong with that woman's back."

Bear cast her a sideways glance while pushing the buttons on the remote. The movie stopped and a sports show popped up on the screen.

"Is there anything wrong with her?" she asked and rolled her eyes at her twin.

"Not a damn thing." His words were light and his tone wistful.

"Hey, Romeo. You have to testify against her, you know."

"Huh? What? Yeah...yeah. Sure. I know that." His voice grew distant.

Oh dear. Maybe sending in the kid was a bad idea.

The men on the television yell-talked at one another about the last hockey game. Mike said something.

"Huh?" She snatched a chip from Bear's hand. The bowl was too far away.

"That necklace Robert always wore. What's it look like again?" Mike asked.

"Kind of like the outline of a diamond shape with two lines sticking out. I always thought it looked a little like a crude vertical fish drawing, stickman style. He said it was a Viking rune for something. Wore it with a gaudy thick chain. Why do you ask?"

"I thought I saw something similar on someone else, but I must've been wrong."

"He got it from his mother, so it's unlikely. Or plot twist, maybe Robert has a half sibling from his mom having an illicit tryst."

"Is that a possibility?"

"Probably not. His mother rarely had a hair out of place." Raven tried to shake the bitterness trying to seep into her chest. Robert's mother had never approved of her and made her opinion of Raven known. Often.

"You and I both know it's always the strict, strait-laced ones that have the most surprising closets," Mike said.

He had a point. The face of her boss, Dan, flashed in her mind. While Dan looked like he might've killed a bunch of people and stashed their bones in his closet, Raven actually had killed someone. Appearances were deceiving.

"Are you still on for tailing Kelly tomorrow?" She had to work at the diner, but Mike booked off so they could close this case.

"You bet!" Mike's over eager voice preceded the dial tone.

They needed to work on his phone etiquette.

Bear and Rourke watched her stuff the phone back in her pocket. Rourke popped another chip in his mouth and chewed loudly. Bear had stocked up on her favourite kind, but she hadn't had any yet. At least, not of that flavour. The moment the big, bad weapon-warping assassin from the Shadow Realm tried one, he snatched the bowl and kept it glued to his lap. He snarled when she reached for a chip, so she let him have the rest. He probably didn't get out much. Her mouth watered at the memory of the savoury bacon and sour cream flavour. Another time, chips. Another time.

"Did you send our baby brother to a peeler bar?" Bear asked.

"I can't figure out what's more disturbing," she said. "Making plans for my baby brother to go to a strip club or not finding it weird I'm making plans for my baby brother to go to another strip club."

"If it's any help," Rourke piped up and chomped on another chip. "I find all you regs incredibly disturbing."

She shook her head. "Not helpful at all."

Rourke shrugged. *Crunch. Crunch. Crunch.*

Odin's balls, he finished the whole bowl.

"What's up with Robert's necklace?" Bear asked.

"Mike thought he saw something similar."

Rourke's gaze snagged on her chest.

She looked down. Her not-black-spinel necklace absorbed the light from the room. "Do you know what this is?" she asked him. He already knew about the necklace because he filched it for Cole, but that wasn't her question.

Rourke's expression grew grim. Potato chips fell from his mouth and decorated his shirt. "It's hard to mistake the Raven's Eye."

Chapter Twenty-Six

"You can kid the world, but not your sister."

~ *Charlotte Gray*

Raven and Juni stared at the black jewel on their mom's kitchen counter while Pepe bleated outside the window begging for food. Chicken simmered in the slow cooker on the countertop and the warm air carried scents of roasted meat and vegetables and made Raven's mouth water.

"Doesn't your science textbook say something?" Raven used her forefinger to poke the rock.

"I'm in grade ten. We don't even cover rock stuff this year." Juni pulled out her phone and scanned the

211

screen. Her headband kept most of her red frizzies from her face while she looked down. "Besides, we have the internet. So far, we know it sinks in water, doesn't fog easily when we breathe on it and doesn't crack or shatter when heated. We couldn't test its refractivity very well because of its colour. At least that's what we're assuming because the test didn't really work. And we're running out of time. Mom has to take me back to the gym soon."

Trust her sister to help her determine the gem's unknown identity in the middle of a volleyball tournament. Juni might be full of snark and raging hormones, but she harboured an inner geek and a passion for shiny things. If Raven didn't know any better, she'd think her sister was a raven shifter like her instead of a fox.

Mike skipped down stairs whistling and bounded into the kitchen. He leaned over Raven's shoulder. "What are you doing to your not-black-spinel?"

"Testing it," Juni answered. She reached into the cupboard and snagged a snack bar. Instead of eating it, she shoved it into the front pouch of her sweatshirt.

"For what? Rabies?" Mike asked.

"No, jerk," Raven said. "To figure out what it is. Rourke called it the Raven's Eye."

"The Raven's Eye?" Mike frowned. "Sounds like something from one of those online games."

She slipped the necklace back on, the weight of the stone against her breastbone familiar and welcome. "Stop talking like you have no experience with gaming, you nerd."

Mike shrugged. "Takes one to know one."

"You're right, though. It does sound like an object with attributes to boost combat ability."

Mike nodded. "The question is. Does it give you +10 dex or +25 str?"

She punched him in the shoulder.

"Ow!" Mike rubbed his arm. "What in the Underworld was that for?"

"Well?"

"Well, what, you psycho?" He scowled at her and continued to rub his arm.

"You asked a question. Did you notice an increase in my dexterity or strength? Or both?"

Juni snickered.

"I hate you." Mike dropped his hand from his arm. "What did Rourke say about it?"

"Nothing," she said.

"What do you mean nothing? Didn't you ask?" Mike reached for a nearby apple.

"Of course, I asked! The fae clammed up faster than a..." She glanced at Juni and cleared her throat. "He refused to say more."

Juni threw up her hands and scowled at Raven.

Mike shrugged and bit into the apple. "You could run a web search."

Raven rolled her eyes.

"Yeah, genius. Like we didn't think of that." Juni reached over and thunked the base of her palm against Mike's forehead.

He swatted her hand away. "Anything?"

Juni and Raven shook their heads in unison. Coordinated sister power. Booyah.

The front door's deadbolt turned, and the door swished open. Supernatural hearing did have some advantages. Mom bellowed from the front entrance, "Juni! I hope you're ready. We need to go."

Juni sighed and slipped her phone back into the pocket of her track pants. "I think it's a diamond."

"What?" Raven's mouth dropped open.

"A diamond. D-I-A—"

"I know how to spell..." Raven pinched the bridge of her nose. "Thanks."

Juni beamed and skipped down the hallway. Her curly red hair swinging in a ponytail as a goodbye.

A diamond? No. That wasn't possible. Some stranger wouldn't gift her a diamond as a tip. And surely Cole would've known if he had it mounted, right? If he did, why didn't he say anything?

Chapter Twenty-Seven

"The average, healthy, well-adjusted adult gets up at seven-thirty in the morning feeling just plain terrible."
~ *Jean Kerr*

L oud thumps down the stairs woke Raven from a delicious fantasy featuring the Lord of Shadows, herself, and no clothes. She enjoyed spending time with her brother and Rourke, but it meant no visit from Cole. And last night, she had to work. She missed him. Like an addict missing her next fix, she craved his touch. Her whole body shook with need, not just for his caress, but for his proximity. Her need for him went beyond the physical stuff. Her texts had gone unanswered, but that meant nothing. At least that's what she told herself. Cell phones didn't work in the Underworld, but that little factoid didn't stop her from checking her phone every five minutes.

Maybe some distance was a good thing.

Mike bounded into Raven's room like a puppy about to get some peanut butter.

"Ugh." Raven rolled over in bed and pulled a pillow over her head. Maybe if she stayed still, he'd go away. "It's too early for this."

"Do you ever see a shark complain its morning? No. A shark goes around eating shit and reminding everyone they're a fucking shark," he said.

"You stole that from a meme."

"Did not."

"Did too."

"Did not. That meme was all about sharks not complaining about *Mondays*. It's Sunday. I was talking about mornings."

"It's still copying."

"This isn't an academic paper. I don't need to cite sources for snarky morning comments. It's almost noon, Rayray. Get up. I want to tell you about my night."

"Ugh," she repeated. While she'd been slogging through another diner shift, moping around and not seeing Cole, Mike had the night off to tail Kelly.

"Did you lose her again?"

A pause. "Yes..."

Raven groaned.

"But once I knew her stage name, a fast web search

gave me her second job site. After I lost her, I headed straight for the club and beat her by five minutes. I don't know why she'd take Boundary. The street is a hot mess right now with all the construction."

Raven slid the pillow off her face and sat up. The scythe rested on the bed beside her and she pulled up the duvet to cover her chest. Sure, she wore a tank top but greeting the cold basement air braless wasn't a show her baby brother needed to see. She blinked a number of times before her blurry vision cleared and she could properly bear the enthusiasm radiating from Mike's face.

She didn't need to see his expression to know he bubbled with excitement. It was all in his voice.

Mike eyed the scythe with a mix of horror and disbelief. "Do I want to know why you're sleeping with a dead woman's weapon?"

Raven pushed the scythe to the side and ignored Mike's comment. "Do I even want to know Kelly's stage name?"

His grin grew.

Nope. She didn't.

"Champagne Delight."

"Honestly. She should've used her first pet name and mother's maiden name." Raven stretched her arms over her head. The delectable aroma of coffee drifted down the stairs into her room. Maybe getting up now wouldn't be so bad after all.

"Then her name would be Pooky Jackson." Mike's smile grew.

"That's one hell of a background check, Mikey."

Mike shrugged. "I added pet names to my checklist because they're often used for passwords."

"That's actually kind of brilliant." She rubbed the sleep from her eyes.

"I got pictures of Kelly going into and out of the back entrance of the club." He handed her a tablet and vibrated with excitement.

She flicked through the pictures. He'd done a great job, clearly capturing her face and the club sign in the same shot. Dressed to impress, Kelly wore a clingy, black wrap dress with a plunging neckline. Her pumps emphasized her toned legs and a silver necklace drew Raven's eye to her ample chest.

Oooo. Shiny.

"Wait a minute." Raven flicked back to a picture that caught her eye and zoomed in. "Is that...?"

Mike nodded. "I thought it looked familiar the other night, but I didn't have any pictures, and didn't get a good look at it. I made sure to get a close up of her necklace last night. It's an exact match to your description."

The pendant on the end of a long silver chain laughed back at Raven, mocking and taunting her like the missing piece of a puzzle she'd been trying to solve.

"Think it's just a coincidence?" Mike asked.

"If it was a cross or a Saint Christopher or something common like that, then probably, but this isn't. Robert told me it had been a gift from his mom. He never took it off. Ever."

"Kelly didn't take hers off, either. Everything else hit the stage floor except the jewellery."

"Ew. I could've gone through life without knowing that and I would've been fine, thank you." Her face screwed up all on its own.

"So judgmental."

"No. I don't like thinking about my baby brother and naked women."

Mike snorted.

"Speaking of that. Did you observe her dancing at the second location as well?"

Mike nodded, grin uncontained.

Of course, he did. Why did she bother asking these questions anymore?

"I think we have enough evidence to go to worker's comp. We'll call them tomorrow and report our findings."

"That's not all I've got."

Oh goodie. More crucial information pre-coffee. "Are you sure this can't wait?"

"I did a little digging to find out more about your unknown black rock of questionable origin. You're right. A straight search didn't yield any results, almost as if someone tried to bury the information." Mike's glower told her exactly how he felt about that.

"Did you discover anything?"

Mike stared at her.

Of course, he did.

"I had to get a little creative, but yes." He pulled out his phone to pull up his notes. Must be good. He was personally delivering the information again. "The Raven's Eye is the largest monocrystalline black diamond in the world at 34.29 carats. It doesn't refract or reflect light like a normal diamond and has an adamantine lustre, instead. The last known sale of the gem was in 1965 for three-hundred-and-fifty thousand dollars, but its current value is estimated at two point one million."

Raven's mouth went dry.

Mike continued. "The origin of the diamond is unknown as is its current whereabouts. It is believed to hold immense power that can only be wielded by someone of Other decent, specifically someone with corvid energy."

All thoughts fled from Raven's mind. What the actual fuck? Why would some random Other gift her an incredibly rare and ridiculously valuable gemstone? That only she could wield? Unease gnawed at her gut.

"Well, I'm not sure I'm ever going to top this tip." Oh good. She could still form words.

"Do you think he was unaware of its worth? Maybe he thought it was a black spinel," Mike said.

"Rourke said it was hard to mistake. I think it's safe to assume anyone from the Underworld would recognize it." Bane certainly had.

"You have enough money to quit your diner job and go to school full time. Why do you look like you've sucked on a lemon?"

She took a deep breath and searched for the words to explain her unease. "Cole saw the stone twice. Once on the night I got it and a second time when he had Rourke steal it and set the stone in a necklace for me." She held the rock up to her face. The light absorbing surfaces had no answers for her.

"And he didn't tell you."

She shook her head. "He didn't want me to know its true value."

"But why?" Mike gathered the photos.

"I'm not sure but he's done nothing but try to protect and shield me from the Underworld. I don't think his motives are nefarious."

Mike grumbled.

She glared.

"Okay, I agree. But I'd still like to know why your ignorance was beneficial in this instance."

She continued to glare.

Mike rose his hands in mock salute. "I agree with you. I really do. I just don't see how not telling you protects you, unless..."

"He didn't want me to sell it," she finished his thought. Cole knew how strapped for cash she was. Her first coherent thought after Mike prattled off the estimated worth was cashing it in.

"He doesn't want me to sell it," she repeated her thoughts and held up the rock again. Her dark essence perked up and the beady-eyed attention of the raven conspiracy she hoarded within zeroed in on the light absorbing surface.

"If Cole's recent actions have all centered on your safety..." Mike nodded at the necklace. "Then the most likely explanation is the Raven's Eye is tied to the same objective somehow."

"It protects me," Raven said.

Mike nodded.

"The real question is how?"

Chapter Twenty-Eight

"Our lives may not have fit together, but ohhh did our souls know how to dance."

~ *K. Towne Jr.*

Energy tethered around Raven and tugged, potent and familiar. Cole. As if he'd heard their discussion, the Lord of Shadows sent his energy forward through the realms to tap her power. The energy knocked against her senses. Oh, this was some sort of magical love tap, or was it just a knock on the door?

She gathered the energy and pulled.

Nothing happened.

She tried again.

Nothing.

Mike said something about metal glowing, but she ignored him, his words drowned out by the thrum of power pulsing in her veins.

Oh for fuck's sake. What did she need to do? Why couldn't there be a Dark Arts for Dummies book out there?

The shadows in the room gathered into a small tornado of darkness. Her scalp prickled with the increasing culmination of Underworld energy.

Mike groaned and snatched the tablet from her hands. "Later."

He left the bedroom and closed the door behind him.

Cole formed in the center of the room. Today, he wore his court clothes—black matte armour with shining silver details, a long flowing cape with a mind of its own, and matching gauntlets, vambrace and boots. His intoxicating scent curled around her.

Raven's mouth watered.

He'd styled his ink-dark hair back and his skin shone with ethereal brightness.

Good thing she wasn't standing.

"Well," he said. "That was better. You recognized my incoming portal. Did you...try to hug it?"

"Yeah." She sat up and flung back the sheets. "I didn't know what to do."

"You will with time."

"That's what I'm afraid of."

"What?"

"Time. I don't have much left."

He cocked his head sideways. Her fear amused him somehow, but she failed to see how or why. His gaze flashed with streaks of silver as if an internal war waged inside. The look was gone in an instant, replaced with heat and need so intense it stole her breath away.

Thank Odin's shriveled nuggets, Mike made himself scarce. "My brother thinks I'm moving too fast with you."

"Which one?"

"Mike." Bear didn't know enough to disapprove, or if he did, he'd remained silent. He hadn't shared much about his relationship with Chloe, either.

Cole nodded. "He doesn't trust me."

"You are a dark fae lord. We all grew up with the stories." Although a number of dark fae attacked mortals with wild abandon the moment the barrier fell, a large faction remained aloof and let the mortals come to them. Instead of using might and power to conquer a weaker party, they used seduction and promises of ecstasy to enslave the easily led. Banshee's tit, even Bane acknowledged other options for waging war aside from violence existed.

Cole's lips twitched and he stepped forward. "I am feared by many and for good reason, but I am not the Lord of Lies and deceit."

"Just assassins."

His smile was vicious. "Who I will ruthlessly deploy

to protect you."

"Why?"

"You know why," he said.

"You barely know me." Well, he knew certain parts of her very well. Raven never developed feelings this intense or this fast in previous relationships.

"I know all I need to know. I know how I feel when I'm with you."

She stood up and faced him. "And how's that?"

"Like myself."

She sucked in a breath.

His words hung in the air. Whatever she expected that wasn't it. What had she expected? Flowery poetry? Compliments? Somehow, his simple response cut to her heart cleaner and sharper than any of the other options.

He ran his hands along her arms and shoulders to cup her face. "I lost myself in the shadows. I had grown accustomed to the darkness. When I walked into that diner, everything changed. You found a way to pull me out."

"Actually, you tracked me down, abducted me and then offered me a deal so you could use me as bait and lure my twin brother out of hiding."

"Memories I will cherish." His smile blinded her.

"Did you orchestrate the customer to give me the Raven's Eye?"

His gaze dropped to the priceless gemstone nestled against her cleavage. His expression told her the truth before he said a word. "Yes."

"Who was he?"

Cole frowned and clamped his mouth shut as if the question legitimately stumped him. "Niall, the Underworld equivalent of my steward, I guess. I wouldn't trust anyone else with such a task."

Huh. She'd heard the name once before, but she'd spent more than one night at Cole's place and never met Cole's steward. Did Cole pick out his steward's "human" attire, or did Niall prance around in dad sweaters in the underworld on his downtime?

Focus, Raven! What did Cole's employee have to do with the necklace, besides act as the delivery mechanism? Argh. "Does the Raven's Eye protect me?"

"Yes."

"Why didn't you tell me?"

"I feared you would sell it."

She had other questions. Important questions. But she'd ask them later. She rose on her toes, gripped the edges of his armour and kissed him. He tasted of sin and coffee.

His hard stance and tense muscles relaxed, and he gathered her in his arms. He deepened the kiss and picked her up. She clung to him, wrapping her legs around his armoured waist. Instead of walking across the room to her bed, he slammed her against the nearest wall.

"That night." He talked between kissing her lips, face and neck. "That night I pinned you to the dirty wall in the alley." More dizzying kisses. "I wanted to do this."

"Even back then?"

He leaned down to suck her nipple through the thin tank top. "Especially then, but even more now. I can't get enough."

She let her head fall back to the wall.

He gripped her undies and tore them from her body.

"I liked those."

"I'll buy you new ones."

All complaints for her ruined panties fled, now consumed with a desperate need to feel him inside her. His hard shaft remained beneath a layer of armour.

"You're too dressed for this."

Cole grinned, his lips travelling along her skin. Shadows wrapped around her, caressing and holding her in place while Cole stepped back and stripped. The cape flowed to the floor, a whisper of fabric on the carpet. The armour followed and clanked on the floor.

He was gorgeous.

Now naked, and glorious, he watched her instead of stepping back into her heat.

The shadows moved to circle her breasts. With increasing pressure, they teased her nipples like phantom hands and teeth. Pleasure rippled through her body.

The shadows continued to stroke her as stronger, wider bands, held her splayed on the wall, open and exposed. Vulnerable to Cole's watchful gaze. He continued to stand, rigid, hard and shaking with need. His gaze raked her body and without words, she knew he loved what he saw.

"Exactly how much of what your shadows touch do you feel?" she panted.

"Everything." His shadows dipped lower, spreading across her thighs, caressing with undulations until they drove upward, straight to her core.

She cried out. Pleasure burst from her as Cole's shadows filled her and expanded.

He drew them in and out and watched the stroking fire burning within her.

The pressure built. She cried out again and suddenly Cole was there. All of him. Wrapped in his arms, real flesh filled her and stretched her and moved within her, riding the aftershocks of her orgasm.

He gripped her thighs and thrust into her, hard, again and again.

Her first orgasm faded only to have her nerves shatter all over again when another, more powerful, wave of ecstasy rocked her.

Cole grunted and pumped into her. He rested his face in the crook of her neck and held her. They panted in unison, dragging in gulps of air, her body clenching around him.

He'd rocked her body like an earthquake and the aftershocks showed no signs of easing up.

She clung to him, not wanting to move, not wanting this moment to end. But he couldn't hold her against the wall indefinitely. Eventually, reality would crash back.

Right now, though, the dark fae Lord of Shadows

held her in his arms and chased away all her fears and insecurities.

No wonder he was addictive. She felt invincible in his arms.

Chapter Twenty-Nine

"You're nuts, but you're welcome here."

~ *Steve Martin*

aven stumbled up the stairs. Exhaustion weighed down her feet. After she recovered from the wall sex, Cole insisted she practice forming portals and then practice accepting and denying his portals. Eventually "accepting his portal" morphed into something kinkier and when she finally found her breath again, she glanced at the clock and realized Sunday dinner was an hour away.

Cole had laughed at her when she pushed him away and insisted he go home to clean up and arrive by the front door. She scoured her body in the shower until her skin turned red to hide her afternoon activities from her family, but in reality, they probably knew exactly what she'd been up to all day, but trying not to flaunt it seemed like the right thing to do.

"Ah, Rayray. There you are." Dad greeted her when she walked into the kitchen. "I have some info for you for the Edwards case."

"You went to work on a Sunday?"

His gaze slid away. "We decided to go out for the day after your...guest...arrived. Mike's suggestion."

Her cheeks burned. "Oh."

Well, at least they weren't in the house to hear all the random sounds Cole got her to make. "Ah. Thanks."

Dad nodded. "It's a good thing Juni had a volleyball tournament."

She perked up. "How'd they do?"

"Lost in the final. Juni's dark on it because her missed serve gave the other team the winning point."

"Balls."

He nodded. "That's the game, though. We keep telling her to practice her serve, but she's so stuck on wanting to be the best hitter."

"But the serve is the most important part of the game. If you don't get it over, you can't win."

They sighed in unison, wordlessly agreeing.

"Anyway. Maybe...next time...you two could go to his place?" Dad suggested.

Oh, look. Her face was on fire again. "Sure, Dad."

He flashed a quick smile and checked the steaming vegetables. The aroma of garlic and herbs infused the kitchen.

Mike bounced into the room and peered over her shoulder at the stove top. "Almost ready?"

Raven spun to her younger brother. "Exactly how did you inform our loving parents and impressionable sister I had a guest?"

Mike laughed and slipped past her. He maneuvered closer to an escape route. "Relax. It was only me and Dad. Mom had already left with Juni for the tournament."

He pulled the fridge open and grabbed a beer. He pointed the can at Raven first.

She shook her head.

Mike shrugged and passed one to Dad.

"Stop deflecting," Raven said. "What did you say?"

Dad cleared his throat and a faint blush coloured his cheeks. "He said the Lord of Dong had arrived and we should leave."

She pinned her brother with her best death glare. "I'm going to fucking kill you."

"No murders before Sunday dinner," Dad said.

After they ate, she'd kill him.

Mike grinned, cracked open a can of beer and shut the fridge door with his foot. "No, you won't."

Gah. He was right. "I hate you."

"No, you don't."

Argh. She spun on her heel to set the table.

A familiar tingling nagged her senses. She

straightened and dumped the cutlery on the table. Similar to Cole's but different. Yet familiar. Without thinking, she grabbed the energy and pulled forward. A portal snapped open in front of her and a wave of fae energy blasted into the room. A conspiracy of ravens flew out of the gap between worlds, flapping their wings furiously and scattering through the room.

Her stomach clenched. The seductive lure of corvid essence wound around her. *Come play*, it called.

When the energy and feathers cleared, Bear stood in front of her with his arm draped over Chloe's shoulders. The birds perched around the room on windowsills and chairs.

"Rayray," her twin greeted her.

Her mouth dropped open.

"You're not the only one who leveled up." He winked.

She snapped her mouth shut and punched his arm. "Why didn't you say something about this on Friday?"

"And ruin this moment? You look like you ate a Sefton beetle."

How in Odin's nutsack did he know about the Underworld dung beetles? And why was he leaving the birds in the dining room. Mom would have a fit. "I hate you."

"No, you don't." Bear shrugged, the movement almost identical to Mike's. Though they had different biological fathers, little moments like that drove home how alike the two men were. "I thought we weren't discussing Otherworld crap. You didn't say anything to me."

Ugh. Typical Bear. He never made the first move when it came to confiding.

Bear spotted Mike over his shoulder guzzling a beer. "Any for me?"

Mike grunted and Bear walked over for some brotherly conversation—placing Raven automatically on mute, apparently.

"Hey, Chloe," she greeted Bear's guest and Cole's sister.

"Hello, Branwen. Will my brother be joining us?"

Apparently, everyone knew about her love life. That wasn't embarrassing. No. Not at all. "Yes, I believe so."

Chloe grinned, her stark white teeth contrasting with her ebony skin. "The Underworld is abuzz with stories of Odin and Cole supporting and protecting the new Corvid Queen."

"Really?" Finally, a source of information who seemed willing to talk.

Birds hopped along the backs of the dining chairs and watched the food with their beady eyes. Bear turned to them and a wave of energy passed between the birds and him. They stopped eying the food, but didn't leave, either.

Dad snapped his fingers. "I almost forgot. I have some information on the Edwards case."

Arghhhh. Dad! Not now. She smiled at Chloe, made a mental note to grill her later about the Underworld, and turned to her father. "What did you find?"

"I ran all the usual background checks and came up with nothing on Robert except his bankruptcy filing, but this time I went a little farther. I called my friend at the station. The police investigated your ex fifteen years ago for the grisly murder of his high school sweetheart."

"What? How could you miss that?" She winced. Her tone came out a little more accusatory than intended.

A raven croaked.

Dad's expression grew grim. "I know. I should've investigated him more thoroughly. I'm sorry I missed it. The information never came up on my searches because he was never convicted, let alone charged. The notes on the file indicate he was a person of interest until the autopsy results came back."

She walked over to the screen door and slid it open. Cool air gushed in and the sound of rain splattering against the deck filled the kitchen and dining room. Pepe bleated and stepped onto the wood planks, his hooves a staccato clip-clop.

"Sorry, buddy. You can't come in." Raven turned to Bear. "The birds?"

Her twin scowled.

"If they poop on the china, Mom's going to kill you."

Bear cringed and flicked out his fingers. The birds croaked and one by one launched from their perches and flew outside. Raven slid the door closed, blocking the sounds of fluttering wings, Pepe's whining and the pitter-patter of rain.

She turned to Dad. "Can you get a copy of the autopsy notes?"

"Already done. The analysis indicates she bled out from wounds inflicted by an animal."

An animal attack? But that would mean... "Shifters?"

Dad nodded.

"A shifter killed Robert's sweetheart and he went on to date two shifter women?"

Mike's face twisted.

"He didn't know you were a shifter." Bear pointed his beer at her. Bear reached into the fridge and held out another one to Chloe. She shook her head and a small shudder wracked her lithe body. Not a fan of Mortal Realm brew, apparently.

"Still weird," Raven said.

"Maybe he doesn't know his fiancée is a shifter, either," Mike said. "She hasn't been forthcoming with that information."

"Did he ever mention the dead girlfriend to you?"

"Don't think so." Raven shook her head. "What was her name?"

"Lenore."

Raven shook her head again. "He rarely spoke about high school. I assumed he wanted to forget that period of his life like everyone else."

"Speak for yourself," Bear said. "By the way, that thing you asked me?"

"Yeah?"

"Large payment about six months ago to a shell company. I haven't tracked the source of the company yet."

Raven ignored Dad's knowing glare from the kitchen and focused on Bear's information. The timing of the payment lined up with Robert refinancing his home, which meant he most likely took money from his equity to make the payment and then started attending a monthly rendezvous. What did that money buy her ex?

What are you up to, Robert?

Before she could voice the many questions running around her head like feral squirrels, otherworld energy tingled against her skin. She identified the fae lord right away—Cole.

With a tug, she accepted the portal and it opened somewhere outside their home.

"Cole's here," she announced.

"Better hurry," Mike said. "You don't want to keep the Lord of D—"

Two steps and a solid punch to Mike's gut shut him up long enough for her to escape the kitchen. Laughter roared behind her as she stalked to the front door.

"I hate you all," she yelled over her shoulder.

"No, you don't," a chorus replied.

The light tinkle of Chloe's bell-like giggle trailed after her.

Chapter Thirty

"Take time to deliberate; but when the time for action arrives, stop thinking and go in."

~ *Andrew Jackson.*

A cold autumn winter wind blew through the trees and threatened to freeze her conspiracy. After discussing the Edwards and Clementine cases, Raven, Mike and their father decided they should investigate the puzzling Wednesday meetings with the Mystery Man before informing Kelly's employer and worker's comp of her fraudulent activities and tipping her off about their surveillance. They wanted to know what Robert was up to.

Dad hadn't been pleased with Raven for going to Bear to illegally access information, but the oddest thing was watching the war between pissed off and proud carryout across his face. The pride wasn't for Raven, either. Bear impressed Dad with his sleuthing skills.

Fast forward to now, Raven rode the tailwinds while freezing off her tail feathers.

When Kelly didn't make the turn toward the café, Raven perked up. Maybe this wasn't a waste of time after all.

Kelly's car continued down Hastings and took the exit to the now-fallen Second Narrow's bridge. Where in the Underworld was she going?

Kelly made a couple more turns and slowed down.

Raven's birds perched on nearby trees and watched the stripper-teacher park the car and walk into a large, newly built home. Raven itched to get closer, but memory of the Other energy blocker sent unpleasant shivers through her collective bird bodies. She'd have to get Mike and see if he could get closer.

She drew her birds in. The dark energy spiraled around her, demanding yet desperate to do her bidding. The world tilted and reformed as she directed her essence back to the house. The shifting energy of the scythe called to her from the corner of the room. Her awareness for the weapon continued to expand over longer distances.

When her vision cleared and her stark basement bedroom walls stopped spinning, she opened the door and yelled up the stairs. "Mike!"

"What?" he yelled back.

"Get your stuff. I'm taking you to Hastings-Sunrise."

"What part?"

In his defence, she'd named a fairly large area. "The part near Montrose Park. The section that borders Burnaby Heights." Raven threw on the nearest outfit, shoved her phone in her pocket and waited for her brother to bounce down the stairs. His feet thumped against each step with the grace of an awkward rhinoceros.

"What's up?" he asked.

"Kelly went to a house, not a café. The street was packed with parked cars."

Mike paused, brow furrowed. "It's not the second Wednesday of the month."

"I know. Maybe they called a special meeting. Maybe these events happen more often, and Robert only attends them once a month. I don't know. What I do know is it's Wednesday and shit is going down in that house."

"Some sort of large scale meeting for fraudsters anonymous?"

"Or something more sinister. I can't risk that they'll have one of those jammer things, so you need to come with me."

Mike recoiled. "What if their weird anti-supe mojo works on mortal shifters, too?"

"It latched onto my Other energy, so I don't think it

will affect you, but if it does, I'll pull you back to safety." She flashed her teeth at him. See? She could be reassuring when she needed to be.

He grunted.

Okay. There were major holes in that bucket, but they didn't have time to dawdle. She opened her arms. "Ready?"

"Wait. You're portalling us there?"

"Come on." She flapped her outstretched hands at him. Why did he look nervous? "It will be fine. I've been practicing."

Mike hesitated.

Her phone vibrated in her pocket. "Hold on." She dug out her phone. "Hello?"

"He's missing again." Sarah's voice was flat, like a sociopath calmly explaining how they planned to commit their next murder.

A chill ran up Raven's spine. "Robert?"

"Yes, Robert," she hissed. "Who else?"

Raven ignored the other woman's tone. "Have you tracked him using the finding app?"

Sarah cursed and hung up.

Okay, then. Hopefully, Sarah would call Raven back when she had a location. Raven stuffed the phone back in her pocket and turned to Mike.

He scowled at her but stepped into her arms.

"There, there, little brother." She patted his back and called for her energy. "It will be okay."

The world disappeared and reformed. Mike pushed away and staggered out of her arms. He lurched to one side and puked into the nearby ditch. After he straightened and wiped his mouth with his sleeve, he glared at her. "Let's never do that again."

She raised her eyebrows and desperately tried to ignore the waft of vomit in the air. "You're going to walk home?"

Mike's face paled.

Before she could reassure him or compliment herself on successfully transporting another person without losing clothing or limbs, her phone vibrated.

Sarah. Again.

Raven held up her finger at Mike and answered the call.

"I got a location," Sarah said.

"Let me guess." Raven scanned the house Kelly had walked into moments ago and prattled off the street address.

Silence met her.

Raven waited.

"How did you know?" Sarah asked finally.

"A hunch."

"Are you there with him?" Her voice dripped acid.

Oh, wow. Back to the accusations. And here Raven thought they'd moved past that. "Not with him. Your case crossed over with another one of our cases."

"Explain."

"I can't. Not yet. I followed my other target to the same location and suspe—"

"They're fucking each other?" Her teeth gnashed over the phone.

Raven took a deep breath and relaxed her grip on the phone, so she didn't crush it. "No, actually. I don't think Robert is cheating on you with another woman."

"A man?"

"An organization." Since witnessing Richard meeting with Kelly's contact, the thought kept coming back to her over and over to the point she could no longer deny it. Why else would Robert, Kelly and their associates have these frequent secret meetings and an object of power that targeted Other energy? They belonged to an organization of some kind. The only question remaining was which one.

But Raven had an idea about that, too, thanks to Bane. He'd gnawed at her ankles like an attack trained Chihuahua to block non-Others from traveling to the Underworld. In addition to this, he'd voiced dislike and concern for Closers. His behaviour nailed her suspicions home—as she'd noted many times in her life, coincidences didn't exist for her. The Closers, Richard, Kelly, these meetings and the energy blocker...they had to all be related.

"An organization?" Sarah's sneer came through in her tone.

"I think Richard and my other case are somehow involved with the Regulators, maybe even the Closers."

Sarah gasped. She didn't speak.

Raven glanced at her screen to check the connection. Still good. Her phone provider hadn't dropped the call.

"That makes no sense," Sarah whispered.

"I agree. I shouldn't have said anything without more proof to back it up." She really shouldn't have said anything until she knew for certain. Stupid! What a rookie mistake.

Mike shook his head at her.

Yeah, yeah, yeah.

"I'm coming," Sarah said.

"No!" Raven barked. "No, you're not. Please stay—"

A dial tone replied.

Damn it! That's all they needed. A hot-headed shifter blowing their cover. They wanted to observe Kelly and Robert before Kelly discovered she'd been investigated and tipped off her co-conspirators they'd been compromised. They held off on reporting their findings to worker's comp for the possibility of discovering what happened at these meetings.

She cursed again. "We don't have much time."

"Willful client?" Mike asked, damn well knowing the answer.

She glared at him.

Mike smirked. "I'm going to walk past the house. If I collapse in agony, please send help."

She rolled her eyes and pushed him forward. He walked out from behind the car shielding them from view and strolled past the house. She held her breath. Her heart pounded so hard, her hearing was consumed with the thumping and the sound of Mike's shoes hitting the pavement.

What the hell were they thinking? Sure, Mike was an adult, but he was also her baby brother. Why had she brought him? Why had she put him in danger? They had no idea what was in that house.

Why couldn't life have a rewind button?

She balled her hands into fists and waited.

Nothing happened.

Mike sauntered past the house and continued down the block. He turned the corner and Raven let out a long breath.

Her phone vibrated again. For fuck's sake. Trying to work here. What did that crazy lady want now? She pulled it out and glanced at the screen.

Mike texted: *Easy.*

Cocky brat.

An hour later, a number of average-looking people exited the house and casually dispersed to various cars. Raven leaned against a nearby streetlight and pretended to play on her phone. From the reflection off her screen, she watched Kelly get in her car and drive off.

"I don't see why we have these meetings during the day," a familiar voice that made all sorts of eye-muscles twitch travelled down the steps and grated her nerves. Robert. "I think she suspects."

Another man chuckled. A quick glance confirmed Robert spoke to the Mystery Man from the coffee shop. He locked the door and walked down the steps with Robert.

Raven slipped behind the van. Her feet scuffed the pavement. Only one person in that house would recognize her and he headed in her direction.

"She probably thinks you're banging someone else. You never could keep it in your pants." Thin and whiny, Mystery Man's voice fit his face perfectly.

"That's even worse! You know who her father is. Think of what they'll do to me."

Say what now? Who was Sarah's father? Surely, Dad's background check would've found something. The report he gave them said Sarah's father was a bank teller.

"They'll do nothing." A vehicle door clicked opened and something thumped inside. If only Raven could turn and get the plate number or the make and model. Damn it. She should've told Mike to take a video as he strolled down the block. They could've reviewed the tape later and pulled vehicle information.

Come on, Mike. Take some pictures. She quickly texted him.

Robert grumbled.

"The supernatural will get what they deserve and when we're through with them, they will be too broken to go after you."

The door shut and the engine turned over. The vehicle travelled away from where Raven hid.

Robert sighed somewhere behind her.

She froze. He hadn't left with the man. Should she let him go?

After today, they'd know someone followed Kelly. Her ex might go into hiding or have time to get his answers straight. This was her chance. Her only chance. Sarah presumably headed here right now to

247

confront him and blow away any cover Raven had.

Take the chance, Crawford.

It was just her and Robert on this now-empty street. She breathed in deep, straightened and stepped onto the sidewalk from behind the van.

Robert walked away from her on the same side of the road. His dress shoes crunched the loose dirt scattered across the sidewalk. He hunched his broad shoulders and ducked his head down a little against the cold wind. He carried none of the confidence and controlled movement like Cole. What had she seen in this man?

"There's one thing I don't understand, Robert," she said.

Her ex froze. He stood silent, facing away from her as if deciding whether to bolt or talk. Ugh. *Please don't run.*

Robert spun around slowly. He reached inside his jacket.

She tensed and grabbed her Other energy. Would he pull a gun on her? Did he even own a gun? Or know how to use one?

From the protective pocket of his jacket, he took out an amulet with a blue stone. He studied it for a few seconds before gripping it in a tight fist.

Okay, then. Weird.

"What do you want, Raven?" His cold voice lacked emotion.

"I guess I want to know why?"

"Why I hate you?"

So, he did despise her. She hadn't read him wrong a month ago when she ran into him at the hospital and later when he graced her with his presence at the diner. "Yes."

"I hate all of your kind," he said.

"My kind? I'm not—"

"Don't lie to me," he hissed. "I saw you."

Her head snapped back as if he slapped her. "What?"

"I liked you. I thought I might've loved you. I heard whisperings about your family being shifters, but I initially ignored the rumours because they were so nice to me and I never saw anything to support the gossip. And then I saw you change. Like some freak of nature. You're worse than a shifter. You're one of *them* and you lied about it. Like they all do, you surrounded yourself with lies."

"Why do you hate Others?" Besides the obvious. Most regs disliked or distrusted Others due to the whole taking over their reality thing and treating them like minions.

"They killed the only woman I truly loved," he said. "They killed Lenore."

"My dad read the police reports. The evidence indicates a shifter, not an Other. I don't understand this misdirected hatred."

"You're all the same!" he snapped. "You're all supernatural. I hate that term. Should be unnatural. Your time is coming. You'll get what you deserve."

"What I deserve? One shifter's actions do not define

the whole group. Tell me, Robert. Did you plan to financially ruin me before or after you discovered my dirty secret?"

"After. And I would've done more had I the ability back then." He rose his shaking fist, still clutching the blue amulet. The silver chain dangled in the air and sunlight danced off its shiny surface. Something decorated the side of the stone. "But I have some power now."

Oooo shiny.

Focus, Crawford.

"You're going to shake jewelry at me?" Raven crossed her arms.

A van turned the corner down the road and travelled toward them. Good. Witnesses.

"You're not a warlock, Robert. What exactly do you plan to do?" she asked.

Robert smiled and mouthed a word. Blue light flashed from the amulet. Pain exploded in her head. She crumpled to the cold pavement. Her cheek pressed into the gritty surface. The energy blocker. The potent power crashed against her corvid energy as if trying to crush it in an invisible fist.

Raven curled up in a ball and groped for her power. Too close. She was too close to the source. She couldn't move.

A door slid open. Feet hit the ground. People yelled.

"How?" Robert snarled.

"I'm not fae, you idiot," Sarah said. "That shit doesn't work—" Sarah growled. "Come back here, you coward!"

More car doors popped open and slammed shut. Another engine revved. The more distant the sound of the engine, the more the pain subsided.

Footsteps approached, slapping the sidewalk. Someone kneeled beside her. Fuzzy floral perfume floated around her.

"You're full of surprises." Sarah brushed Raven's hair from her face. "What exactly are you that the fae-looking artifact Robert wielded affected you and not me?"

Raven moaned and rolled over. Little rock pebbles stuck to her skin and drool coated half of her face.

Sarah smirked. "Your secret is safe with me, Other."

"I think I have enough information to formally close your case." The air scraped her dry lungs and her mouth filled with the iron taste of blood.

Sarah's smirk spread into a large, toothy grin. "I can't wait to hear what you discovered."

Another van pulled up. Large men jumped out and jogged toward them. Not good.

More fuzzy scents coated the air.

"Yeah." Raven licked her dry lips. "Let's set up a meeting for tomorrow and I'll go over my findings."

Sarah shook her head, her fluffy hair bouncing off her face. "No. I think not."

The men closed the distance. Their slightly furry scents familiar. They waited for Sarah's orders.

Robert's fiancée turned to them. "Robert fled. He's long gone, now."

Not assassins sent to smite either of them, then. That was good news. Maybe?

The bad news was she had no idea what to expect and she hadn't fully recovered from the energy blocker. The effects still ravaged her body.

"No," Sarah continued. "You'll come with me now to make a full report."

The men helped Raven to her feet and guided her to the van. Raven needed a little more time to recover but fear no longer wracked her body. She'd escape these shifters if needed, but she doubted they meant her harm. She may as well see where this led. Their destination wasn't the prominent question in her mind, though.

Where in the Underworld was Mike?

Chapter Thirty-One

"We are all born ignorant, but one must work hard to remain stupid."

~ *Benjamin Franklin*

The jostling van ride was uncomfortable and awkward. Eventually, the effects of the energy blocker wore off. Raven could escape her captors, but she'd already committed to seeing how this played out. She took a risk, but they hadn't bound her or taken out the guns stuffed in their waistbands.

The burly non-verbal driver pulled up to a large mansion off West Marine Drive. The palatial building sprawled over a manicured lawn, surrounded by a cultivated garden. *Bank teller, my ass.*

"Nice house," Raven said. More than nice. It was a fucking palace.

Dark clouds rolled in and covered the afternoon sun, but the weather did little to diminish the intimidating impression of the mansion.

Sarah flashed teeth at her, not quite a smile. "My father's place. He acquired it after the last owner got into a vampire territory feud and lost."

How the hell was she supposed to respond to that? "Nice."

Rain started to pummel the windshield. It bounced off the metal roof as they clambered out of the van. The guards escorted her into the house. The warm, dry entrance greeted her. Strategically placed antique furnishings and rugs emphasized the size of the room and the owner's wallet at the same time.

Sarah leaned in. "The place came fully furnished."

Dead vampire possessions. Raven shuddered and followed the men through the house. Their feet whispered against the rugs and shiny tiles as they led her to an office bigger than her family's living room and kitchen combined.

An older man sat behind a pedestal-style desk made of solid oak. Drapes covered two immense windows behind him, leaving a pair of desk lamps with green shades to illuminate his face. The furry scents of the occupants intensified.

The man, presumably Sarah's father, studied her with his golden, unflinching gaze. The wrinkles lining his face suggested he laughed a lot but right now, he wasn't smiling. He didn't stand to greet them, either.

Recognition clicked. She knew this guy. She knew this smell.

She groaned, Tony the Tooth, leader of the powerful, and less-than-law-abiding hyena shifter gang.

She turned to Sarah. "Your last name is Edwards."

Robert's fiancée flashed more teeth. "Did nothing come up on your background checks?"

Not a fucking thing and she knew it.

Sarah's father stood. Though older, the white dress shirt emphasized a muscular build from years of grappling and busting up peoples' faces. "I spent a lot of money procuring a fake identity for my daughter that would pass the scrutiny of law enforcement. I'm glad it passed the test."

Fuck that. Raven and her father would've dug deep enough, eventually.

"Do you wear something to mask your scent?" Raven asked.

"We all do."

Raven turned to Sarah. "Yet, you told Robert your background."

Sarah stiffened. "I told him nothing."

"He knew," Raven said. "I overheard a conversation between him and the leader of their organization. They mentioned your father."

Tony growled. "I think it best that you give me a full report of your investigation and explain exactly what information my money purchased."

Chapter Thirty-Two

"Never be afraid to try something new. Remember, amateurs built the ark, professionals built the Titanic."

~ *Louis Menand*

Tony's men dropped Raven off unceremoniously at her house. Tony the Tooth had concerns about her silence, but she assured him the contract she signed with Sarah guaranteed her discretion. Raven had nothing to gain. Not to mention Sarah held a secret of Raven's as well. Presumably, Tony and his hyena gang would, too, the moment she left the room.

Raven stomped into the house and paused to enjoy

the burst of warm air on her face. The rain clouds had cleared for now, but they'd be back. She closed the door behind her and called out to her brother.

No response.

"Mike?"

Silence.

Mom and Dad weren't home from work yet. Maybe Mike was at the office with Dad. She'd texted him on the van ride home to let him know she was okay and to tell him to head home. She pulled out her phone and checked her messages. No response.

Dread climbed along her spine. Her fingers flew over the keyboard.

Where are you?

Nothing.

Are you all right?

No response.

ANSWER ME NOW.

No answer. She hit the call button.

"Hi," Mike answered

"Mike, where—"

"You've reached Mike..."

Voicemail.

No!

She gathered her energy and split to reform at the meeting house. She sprinted around the building where she last saw Mike. Following the side street, she retraced the path he would've taken after she lost sight of him and entered the alley.

There!

Mike's phone lay face down on the ground. She plucked the device off the dirty concrete. Unread notifications lined his screen.

Who's Becka?

Mike hadn't mentioned dating anyone.

She wiped the moisture and dirt from the screen. Where was her brother? He'd never voluntarily separate from his phone. What happened to him? Was he okay? Did it have to do with the mysterious girl texting him? Or did one of the meeting members snatch him? Dread clenched her entire body. Her breathing became short and fast.

Slow down. Think. Panic later. What should she do? What could she do? Who could help her?

She pulled a pocket knife from her back pocket, split open her finger and summoned Cole. "Beul na h-Oidhche gu Camhanaich. Come to me."

He materialized in seconds. The shadows clung to him, slowly dripping to the ground, like the last drops of water from a shower. He studied their surroundings and frowned. "Are you okay?"

She forced her breathing to slow down so she could speak. "Someone took Mike."

Cole's gaze flashed. "Can you track his—"

Raven held up Mike's phone.

Cole clamped his mouth shut. The shadows pooled around him and the alley darkened. In broad daylight, it looked like the end of the day. "Where's Rourke?"

Whoops. An invisible knife stabbed her heart. She hadn't given the dark fae a chance to follow her and she didn't grab him when she brought Mike to the meeting location, either. If he'd been with Mike, her brother wouldn't be missing right now.

Darkness clouded Cole's gaze.

"It's not his fault. I'll explain why later, we need to find Mike."

"You'll have to use your power."

"My power? What the hell can I do?"

"When you portal, you've been practicing travelling to familiar places by envisioning the location and how it feels. Now you need to form a portal and travel to a person. Envision Mike and how he feels. Think about what he means to you and how much you love him."

"Why don't you do it? You're better at all of this than me." What if she messed up? What if Mike was hurt? What if...she was too late?

Cole shook his head. "I don't have a blood bond with Mike and he's not actively summoning me."

Fucking Others and their blood fetishes.

"Not only do you share blood with him, you love him. The trip should be quick," Cole said.

A thought pinged in her brain. "If it's so easy, why didn't you portal to your sister when she was missing?"

"I tried. I was blocked. Your twin is not ignorant of our ways. He used a rune to prevent her from portalling and from anyone traveling to her. Had I known the full extent of your powers, I would've taught you to portal sooner and saved us a lot of time. Let's hope whomever abducted Mike has no knowledge of ancient Underworld runes."

"Okay," she said. "I can do this."

"You're taking me with you."

"Absolutely not. Robert had an energy blocker. It was excruciating up close and only half of me is from the Underworld. What if other members of the group have them, too? What if they've laid a trap with Mike as the bait? If I get stuck, you'll know what happened and you're better equipped for a rescue mission."

Cole shook his head. "Non-negotiable. I'm coming with you."

His body tensed. His gaze flashed. He readied himself for an argument.

"Fine." She'd already learned teamwork wasn't the enemy. She pulled out her phone and sent a message to Dad: *Someone took Mike. We followed Kelly and Robert to a meeting house and Mike went missing after going into the alley. He dropped his phone. Cole and I are going to portal to him. I'm leaving his phone in the alley so you can scent track if needed. Love you.*

She sent the address of the meeting house and turned to Cole. "Okay. Let's do this."

She opened her arms and Cole stepped into her heat. His strong arms circled her, and his heady scent and shadows wrapped around them.

"It will work out, Einin," he said, pulling her close. "Close your eyes and think of Mike. Feel your love for him."

Cole's deep voice rumbled over her skin like a lover's caress. She followed his instructions. The world dissolved and dark energy whirled around them.

Chapter Thirty-Three

"Sometimes, you have to get angry to get things done."

~ Ang Lee

Raven and Cole reformed in a cellar. Bands of dark magic dissipated and faded into the shadows of the room. Damp, mouldy air greeted them along with the sound of dripping water. Mike kneeled across the room with his head down and his arms wrenched behind him, chained to the wall at an uncomfortable angle.

"Mike," Raven hissed and ran over to him.

He raised his ginger-mopped head. His eyes widened. "Rayray?"

One eye was severely swollen and already bruised. His lip was split, and one cheek looked puffier than the other. He hadn't shifted into a fox to escape and some weird energy vibrated along the chains that bound him. Shifter chains? They existed?

Molten lava flowed in her veins and her vision stained red. Someone would die for this. "I'm going to kill them."

She didn't even care who the fuck "them" was. It didn't matter. She'd tear them apart. This was her baby brother. This was *Mike*.

"Get the amulet. It's the...the..."

"Energy blocker." She glanced up. There, on a hook by the door, hung a blue amulet similar to the one Robert had held in her face. She ran over and ripped it from the hook. The power of the stone vibrated along her skin, but no waves of pain stabbed at her body. Robert had mumbled something before it activated last time. It must require some sort of trigger spell. Etched into the largest face was the symbol both Robert and Kelly wore on their necklaces.

Chains clanked behind her.

"Thanks," Mike mumbled.

She turned and watched Cole help her brother to his feet. The chains that had bound him lay useless at his feet.

"It's the symbol of Othila." Mike wobbled but stood. He nodded at Cole and the Lord of Shadows released him. "It's a Viking rune that symbolizes the ancestral home passed from generation to generation and the strength of a united family. It also represents separation."

Cole grunted.

"The amulet you're holding with the Othila symbol is very powerful. He wouldn't shut up about it." Mike turned to Raven and swallowed. "He tried to use it on me."

"Who?"

"Robert," Mike spat.

Cole scowled and the lights flickered.

"He spotted me in the alley when he was driving away. The amulet didn't work on me. I'm a shifter, not fae. When that plan failed him, he pointed a gun at me and told me to climb into the passenger seat and throw my phone out the window. His hands shook so much, I thought he'd shoot me by accident."

"I found your phone," Raven said. "Becka says hi."

Mike's cheeks reddened and his expression softened for an instant before it returned to pained determination. "Robert didn't want you tracking me with my phone."

"He's not as dumb as we'd all like him to be," she said.

"He will be nothing after I'm through with him." Cole's dark gaze flashed.

Raven shivered. Cole had killed for her before. "I need you to take Mike back."

"No."

"Yes."

"Please," she said. "I need to know he's safe."

"He's right here," Mike muttered.

Raven ignored her brother and kept her gaze trained on Cole. "You take Mike home. I'll deal with Dr. Douche. You can't protect me forever."

The look on Cole's face said he disagreed.

She sighed. "I'll confront him when you return. Take this with you." She tossed the amulet at him.

Cole snarled, snatched the amulet, and grabbed Mike. His gaze remained locked on her the entire time, as if she'd disappear on him if he looked away. "You do not engage without me."

Mike stumbled and fell into Cole.

Raven rolled her eyes and watched the shadows envelope the men she loved.

Raven gulped. Loved? Oh no. She really had fallen hard for Cole. Love? Her heart spasmed.

Oh crap. She did. She loved that shadow-wielding dark fae assassin. How was that even possible? They hadn't known each other for long. They hadn't been out on a date yet. She wasn't the type to swoon and fall for a guy so fast. The last time she loved it hadn't worked well for her and that had taken almost a year of dating. She thought it had ended badly with her in debt for fifty thousand, but her story with Robert wasn't over. Now she was in his basement after rescuing her brother from his evil clutches.

Her relationship with Cole drastically differed from what she had, or thought she had and ultimately lost with Robert. Cole didn't demand anything from her. He wasn't a leech. He wanted to protect her and gave her the strength and skills and encouragement to stand on her own. He stood back and let her sort out her own problems despite having more knowledge and the ability to step in and bulldoze the entire situation. He gave and gave...and gave.

She shook her thoughts back to the present and turned toward the door. She ran straight into a fist.

Chapter Thirty-Four

"When I am silent, I have thunder hidden inside."

~ *Rumi*

Pain exploded across Raven's face. Her vision went black and an instant headache bloomed behind her eyes. She fell backward, staggering until she caught herself on a support post. Another fist flew toward her face. She lurched to the side, stumbled and fell.

She rolled and a booted foot narrowly missed connecting with her midsection. What the hell?

She scrambled to her feet and faced her attacker. Her sight crystallized and focused. Thick dishevelled brown hair framed a traditionally handsome face. Light brown eyes held ice and hate as a familiar man glared at her.

"Robert," she hissed. "You've sunk to a new low."

Robert snarled and lunged. "You're not a woman to be cherished and protected. You're an animal."

She dodged another strike. When she said he sunk to a new low, she referred to Robert kidnapping and beating up her brother, but if he wanted to add hitting women to his list of character flaws, she'd show him why that was a bad idea. Raven had zero training as a fighter, but she had years of scrapping with brothers. A spoiled brat and an only child, Robert grew up entitled. He didn't have to fight for a thing his entire life.

And his form was horrible.

"Technically, we're all animals," she said. Thank you, Mike for that useless fact. "You're a doctor. Shouldn't you know that?"

"You're a thing. A parasite. We need to stamp your kind from the Mortal Realm."

"Is that what your teabag party was all about?"

"We have the Amulet of Othila. It harnesses Fm"

Fm stood for Force of Magic. The discovery of Fm played a pivotal role in bringing down the barrier between the Mortal Realm and the Other Realms.

"Had."

Robert hesitated, gaze darting to the hook on the wall.

Raven stepped in, delivered the hardest body shot she could throw and darted out of range.

Robert doubled over and wheezed.

Everyone underestimated the power of a well-placed body shot.

Robert gasped for air. "No matter. We also have the Murdoch Manual."

"Because a bigot's bible is going to save you?" Dr. Murdoch wasn't prejudiced, but the group of mortals who coveted her research materials generations after her death were.

"It's not a bible. It's the original lab manual of Gabrielle Murdoch, the lead physicist responsible for the barrier collapse, you simpleton."

Raven rolled her eyes. She knew exactly who the doctor was, but Robert couldn't help talking down to her.

"If those scientists took it down, we can put it back up." Robert straightened, an ugly sneer spread across his face.

How did she ever love him? How did she think she loved him? Despite his classically handsome features, he was an ugly person. Rotten.

"That book won't save you," she said. Any minute now, Cole would return.

"No," he agreed. "But this will." He reached behind him and pulled a small handgun from his waistband.

Seriously. How small was that thing? "Is that a gun or a toy?"

He brought the weapon up.

As soon as he moved, Raven pulled her dark energy and combusted into her conspiracy of ravens. *Target that, bitch.*

Robert's eyes widened. Then narrowed. His mouth tightened and he took aim.

A loud boom punched the air and rebounded against the walls.

Pain erupted through her conspiracy and shared consciousness. Robert had shot one of her birds. Her consciousness reformed to spread over one less bird.

Bastard.

She should flee. She should make a portal and get the hell out of here.

No.

Not again.

She wouldn't run away from Robert and the pain he inflicted again. She had to see this through.

Her conspiracy darted in and swarmed her ex.

Another shot.

More pain.

No turning back. She'd already committed to taking him down.

Her birds tucked their wings in and dove at Robert. He screamed and swatted at his face.

There!

An opening.

The birds pecked at his skin.

Robert screeched and covered his face. Blood splattered the unfinished basement floor.

He batted at the birds. The gun clattered to the ground. Pain erupted across her consciousness as he tried to fight off her birds.

She ignored it.

There was no escape for Robert. He tried to shoot her. But worse. He took Mike. He hurt Mike. There was no redemption for this man.

Dark energy pulled at her. Raven grabbed the power and pulled, reforming in human form. She stood in front of Robert with the Scythe of Corvids in her hand.

How did the weapon get here?

She shook the question away. Another time. He'd taken her brother and beaten him. Mike. Her baby brother.

Roberts's bloody face gaped at her, but only for an instant. Pure, ugly rage consumed any remaining surprise. Robert snarled and lunged. The energy of the scythe vibrated in her hands. She swung and brought the weapon down. Metal reflected light and sliced through skin, tissue and bone. Blood sprayed.

Robert's head slid from his shoulders with a sick, wet thump. His gaze wide. His body went limp and flopped to the floor.

She stood frozen, gripping the scythe as if her life was forfeited if she let go. She killed someone. Again. Her head grew light. She knelt beside Robert's prone, headless body, supporting her weight with the scythe against the floor. Her limbs weighed a ton and her head began to throb. She glanced over at Robert's broken and bloody body.

Odin's pink panties, she killed Robert. *He's dead. Gone.* Images of the headless Corvid Queen resurfaced. Raven's stomach rolled. Her vision swam. She leaned over and threw up.

She continued heaving until well after her stomach had emptied its entire contents.

"You did well, Einin," Cole's voice, soft and gently, spoke behind her. "Did you kill him with the scythe?"

"Yes." She glanced up at hum. Her world tilted and her stomach clenched. "Why do you look like you swallowed a Sefton beetle?"

"You did well," he repeated. "Using the scythe means you've bloodied the blade after bonding to it. In addition to gaining full access to the scythe's formidable magic, you can now complete the ascension to your position as the Corvid Queen and wield the power it grants."

"Again, why do you look so sad?"

"I didn't wish this for you."

Her fingers gripped the smooth shaft of the scythe. "Because I'm not a killer."

"No, you're not. That is why I never mentioned the secret to unlocking the Scythe of Corvids or the true cost of your mantle." Cole crouched beside her, his warmth and shadows offering a soothing silent comfort. "But you did what you had to do to protect those you love."

She turned to him, his expression open, his eyebrows turned up as if he was in pain. Maybe he remembered what drove him to be an assassin.

"Is that why you started killing?" she asked.

"No, Einin." He reached over and helped her stand

with her wobbly legs. "I didn't know love back then."

"Oh."

"I didn't know love until now."

The intensity of his gaze threatened to drown her. He loved her? Had he just said that?

"Don't send me away from you again, Einin. I don't have it in me to leave you so vulnerable." His gaze flicked to the gun resting on the floor to the side of Robert's body and then the scythe in her hand. His shadows wrapped around her. "You were supposed to wait for me."

"Robert didn't get the memo."

Cole glowered at the body as if contemplating reanimation just for the satisfaction of taking Robert's life himself.

She slid her hand up his face and turned his attention back to her. "Robert is gone, and I am safe."

His grip tightened on her arms.

"And you can't go around making sweet proclamations when I just spewed my guts out. I can't kiss you right now."

Cole chuckled and pulled her into the heat of his body. His arms tightened around her. His deep voice fanned her skin as he whispered. "You are everything to me. You are the light chasing the shadows from my heart. You are the reason to my madness and the clarity of my world that's known only chaos."

Since kissing was out, she clung to him instead. She closed her eyes and squeezed, pressing her body against his as hard as possible, hopefully expressing everything in her heart since words had apparently failed her. Sure, she had a lot of questions, and a list of things she needed to figure out, but right now, right here, she didn't need to think. Just feel. Enjoy the press of Cole's body against hers and let her mind drift and dream of possibilities. Reality would crash back soon enough.

Epilogue

"Lord, what fools these mortals be!"

~ William Shakespeare

Raven sat with Mike at the boardroom table with Scott O'Halloran, a representative from Worker's Compensation of British Columbia on one side and Amy Bennet, the superintendent from the school district on the other. Mike wore a long-sleeved shirt to cover his arms. The cast had finally come off, leaving his arm pale with the new skin look. He couldn't hide the yellowing on his face from his healing black eye but at least the swelling along his cheek and jaw had gone down.

With only a tiny scratch on her face, Raven appeared more presentable in dress pants and shirt, but inside she was a mess. Reality had crashed back the moment Cole left her in her basement bedroom. She'd taken another life, she possessed a rare diamond that protected her in some way, and she needed to figure out how to block portals for Bane. When and how she'd find a way to understand or deal with any of these things was very much up in the air, but she had to press pause on that part of her life and deal with the current situation first.

Kelly Clementine walked into the room wearing a blazer, matching skirt and flats. She opted for a fresh makeup free face, probably hoping the bags under her eyes would help her case. The designer perfume she wore filled the room and her union representative trailed into the boardroom behind her.

The WCBC official stood and waved at the seats across from them. "Ms. Clementine." He turned to the union rep. "Max, good to see you again."

"I don't know why you've dragged us to this meeting," the union rep said. "As per Article G.111.1 of the collective agreement, Kelly is entitled to benefits while on medical leave and she dutifully reported the workplace incident."

They sat down. The plastic creaked and the wheels rolled on the protective mat under the table. Kelly winced and squirmed in her chair as if the action hurt her "bad" back. What an actress.

Maybe her ass hurt from all the twerking over the

weekend.

Kelly scanned her audience. Her gaze snagged on Raven and her expression darkened. What the hell? Why did Kelly look like she recognized Raven? They'd never met. Had the teacher-stripper spotted her when she was on stake-out? Maybe Raven had lost her touch.

"Yes, she is," Amy said. "But only if the injury and workplace claim is legitimate."

Kelly and Max stiffened.

The union worker glanced at Kelly. "You need proof. You can't enforce a baseless allegation."

"You are correct again." Scott smiled but didn't convey any warm, fuzzy feelings. "Let me introduce Raven and Mike Crawford from Crawford Investigations, a reputable private investigative firm from Burnaby."

Raven and Mike nodded in unison and turned to Kelly. The woman had pulled out her necklace to play with the Othila rune, a slight smirk playing on her lips.

"Raven, can you please outline what you and your colleague discovered over the course of your investigation?" Scott asked.

Raven let her grin escape and spread across her face. "Gladly."

It took Raven about ten minutes to detail the investigation and the evidence collected—ten minutes to expose Kelly Clementine's lies and bring her world of deceit toppling down. Normally, causing the look of utter devastation across someone's face would inspire empathy and remorse, but Raven had zero fucks to give this Other-hating, resource-leaching bigot.

Kelly's smirk had disappeared.

The superintendent's face fell. Her mouth gaped open and when Raven concluded her summary, Amy turned to Kelly. "Why?"

"What?" Kelly dropped the hands she'd cried behind and sniffed.

"We pay our teachers well."

Kelly snorted. "Our province provides the second lowest pay for teachers across Canada and we have the highest cost of living."

"But still..." Amy looked down at her hands. "I've heard of picking up serving shifts, but stripping..."

"I like it, okay?" Kelly crossed her arms. "I'm good at it, and I make more dancing than I do teaching."

Max, the union rep, looked speechless and horrified at the same time. He hadn't anticipated the breadth and extent of Kelly's betrayal and double life.

"Why not quit, then? Why make a fraudulent claim?" Scott asked. "This is an indictable offense."

Um, duh. The money, dude.

"The money." Kelly swiped at her tears, gaze turning cold. "And I wanted to keep the extended teacher benefits."

The superintendent shook her head.

"I would've got away with it, too, if you hadn't set these disgusting Others on me."

Raven stiffened. How the hell did this bitch know?

Mike laughed. "I'm a shifter, and I didn't need to be in fox form to figure out how dirty you are."

Raven winced.

"For the record, I stayed in human form the entire time," Mike quickly added. "I've had a cast recently removed and medical records will show I was human-bound for the entire duration of this case."

Oh thank goodness he snuck in that tidbit. The last thing they needed was to get dragged into court for the defence to try to discount Mike's testimony and evidence.

"I wasn't talking about you, pest." Kelly sneered and jabbed a finger in the air at Raven. "We know all about you and what you are. We know what you did, and we have the book. We will bring you down."

Raven rolled her eyes and leaned forward. "You'll find that difficult to do when you're in jail."

Raven and Mike pushed away from the table and stood. The WCBC rep and superintendent stood as well to shake their hands.

"Thank you for your services," the WCBC Rep said. "We will forward the payment as agreed upon."

Raven and Mike said farewell and made their way out of the building, leaving Kelly to her fate.

The crisp air greeted Raven as she stepped out onto the sidewalk. Her heels clacked against the stone steps. Though she kept it together in the boardroom, her mind still reeled. *They* knew what she did? *They* knew she killed Robert? What if *they* had surveillance footage? What if she ended up sharing a jail cell with Kelly? What would her parents say? How could she face them if they knew what she did?

"Raven!" Megan waved at her from across the street. Her friend looked both ways and jogged toward them. A necklace slipped from inside her shirt. The sunlight reflected off the metallic surface.

Raven froze. She'd know that rune anywhere.

Her best friend wore the symbol of Othila.

~ The End ~

"And the Raven, never flitting, still is sitting, still is sitting
On the pallid bust of Pallas just above my chamber door;
And his eyes have all the seeming of a demon's that is dreaming,
And the lamp-light o'er him streaming throws his shadow on the floor;
And my soul from out that shadow that lies floating on the floor
Shall be lifted—nevermore!"

~ Excerpt from *The Raven*, by Edgar Allan Poe

Did you enjoy reading Nevermore? Please help this author out and tell someone or leave a review. Your support is much appreciated.

Raven and Cole's story continues in
Queen of Corvids
A Raven Crawford Novel, Book Three.

RAVEN'S LIST OF SERVER PET PEEVES

1. Campers

2. Split cheques for large groups

3. Seagulls

4. Finger snappers and wavers

5. Unwanted comments about appearance

6. Old people with bags of coins

7. Vegans

8. Mysterious gem-toting men

9. Customers grabbing or tugging on serving apron

10. The Smoker Card

11. Penny Tips

GLOSSARY OF TERMS

Mortal: any inhabitant of the Mortal Realm. Note: All entities of all the realms can be killed, but this term is reserved for anyone who is not an Other. Used as a derogatory slur by Others.

Other: Any inhabitant NOT from the Mortal Realm. Any inhabitant from the Realm of Light, the Underworld or the Shadow Realm. Mortal, but not a mortal.

Reg: A "regular" human being from the Mortal Realm without any supernatural powers or skills.

Regulators: An organized group of regs who despise Others and hold meetings to bitch about the unfairness of life.

ROL: Realm of Light. An Other realm full of rollers who look down on everyone else.

Rollers: supernatural beings from the Realm of Light

Underworld: An Other realm, often in direct conflict with the Realm of Light. Contains multiple, smaller realms, such as the realms of War and Lust.

ACKNOWLEDGEMENTS

I'm aware the regulatory branch responsible for managing workplace injury claims is NOT called the WCBC. I changed the name because this is a made-up world and although I try to mirror reality and make events and organizations realistic, they're not actually real. And I don't want to get sued.

I'd like to thank [redacted] for WorkSafeBC for advice and information on how fraudulent claims are handled and how claims are paid via the employer. None of the information provided was confidential or private, but the name of the employee has been redacted to protect them from anyone assuming they conducted themselves unprofessionally. Any liberties I took with portraying the WCBC were exactly that— liberties. I filled in the gaps with what made sense for my world and storyline.

I'd like to thank Karilyn Bentley and Wendy P for beta reading, Lara Parker for her ever-fabulous editing and Tammy Payne for proofreading. I'm so very grateful to this team of supporters who help me improve my stories.

Any errors contained in this book are my own, despite my best efforts to research and consult experts, and everyone's best efforts to steer me in the correct direction.

A HUGE thank you to Anna L. Spies at Eerilyfair Design. I'm pretty sure the majority of my sales are due to her gorgeous artwork, and *Nevermore* happens to be my personal favourite of the three covers.

Most of all, thank you to you, the reader, for trusting me with your precious reading time. I hope you enjoyed this story as much as I enjoyed writing it.

About the Author

J. C. McKenzie is a book-loving, gumboot-wearing, unapologetic science geek. She's the author of the Carus Series, the Obsidian Flame Series and the Raven Crawford Series. Born and raised on the West Coast, J. C. sets the majority of her books in the Lower Mainland of British Columbia, Canada. She writes urban fantasy and paranormal romance with sassy heroines and brutish, alpha-type men.

Visit her at www.jcmckenzie.ca

Amazon: www.amazon.com/author/jcmckenzie
Blog: jcmckenzie.blogspot.ca
Goodreads: www.goodreads.com/JCMcKenzie
Twitter: twitter.com/JC_McKenzie
Facebook: www.facebook.com/j.c.mckenzie.author
Instagram: www.instagram.com/j.c.mckenzie